Margaret Thomson
and has lived in Gla
She is the author of many short stories, her autobiography, *The Making of a Novelist*, and several novels including *The Dark Side of Pleasure*, *Light and Dark* and *Rag Woman, Rich Woman*. The *Breadmakers* trilogy, (*The Breadmakers*, *A Baby Might be Crying* and *A Sort of Peace*) is her most famous work.

Also by Margaret Thomson Davis

THE BREADMAKERS
A BABY MIGHT BE CRYING
A SORT OF PEACE
THE DARK SIDE OF PLEASURE

The Prisoner

MARGARET THOMSON DAVIS

A STAR BOOK
published by
the Paperback Division of
W H Allen & Co Plc

A Star Book
Published in 1989
by the Paperback Division of
W H Allen & Co Plc
Sekforde House, 175/9 St. John Street,
London, EC1V 4LL

First published in Great Britain by Allison & Busby Ltd,
1974

Phototypeset by Input Typesetting Ltd, London

Printed in Great Britain by
Cox & Wyman Ltd, Reading

ISBN 0 352 32251 9

Chapter One

Celia watched the men in the park. She often came to the Botanic Gardens and sat primly yet provocatively, a book on her lap, her slim legs twined and her skirt rucked high enough to display her legs to best advantage.

The serious looking book and the heavily framed reading glasses perched on the end of her nose gave her, she felt, all the protection she needed.

She was, after all, a respectable married woman from the dignified middle-class district of Bearsden. The only thing that brought her to Great Western Road, where the park was situated, was the fact that her husband owned a hairdressing and beauty salon in the area. She came to have her weekly hair-do, manicure and facial. Now fresh from the salon, her black hair a smooth bouffant with curls flicking out at each side of her face, her nails like clusters of rain-glistened rosebuds, and her skin tingling from the massage that preceded the flawless make-up, she felt as if she had been perfumed and prepared as a love offering. She felt like a woman from a harem who awaits the sultan and hopes that when she reveals herself to him he will be pleased with what he sees.

Often she had dreams like that, of swirling, snaking, oscillating like a belly dancer in front of an adoring eastern potentate. Or being pursued by some ardent admirer who kept pleading frantically with her to allow him to make love to her and who trembled at the mere touch of her hand.

But this tuned-up feeling, this ripeness, this keen anticipation was never assuaged. Today for instance she had only her neighbour Mrs Anderson coming for afternoon tea.

Later Peter would arrive home and after his meal he would either say he was exhausted and loll back in his chair watching television all evening or, more than likely, he would bring his partner and friend Owen home for dinner. Then he and Owen would gossip about the customers who had been in the salon or they would discuss new trends in hair styles or colours or equipment and they would do their books and chew over the financial side of the business.

Sometimes they just went out to the garage and tinkered with the car.

The unexpected music of a wolf-whistle jerked Celia into the immediate present. She raised her eyes and tugged down her skirt in a flurry of pleasurable indignation. Then she became conscious of coy giggles beside her and realised that the man approaching was aiming his admiration at a young girl in skin-tight denims and sweater who was sitting at the other end of the bench.

She had not noticed the girl's arrival and now, flicking nervous embarrassed glances sideways at the long blonde hair and unmade-up face, Celia saw that she was about the same age as her daughter Wendy.

"Hi, Babs." The young man's voice was a caress. "You look great. Been waiting long?"

He sat down beside the girl and they melted into one another and began kissing gently, tenderly.

Celia fingered her glasses and tried to concentrate on her book. A rush of tears gusted about inside her. She was nearly forty. Forty!

Another man came and sat down. The bench was not big and it was a crush with the four of them. The man's thigh lay warm and heavy against hers. Desperately she studied her book and prayed that he did not feel the pulse that was beginning to drum through her veins and vibrate the bench and the ground underneath it. The man moved his arms smoothly but with a concentrated stealth that was almost a tremble. From the corner of her eye she noticed the raincoat that he had folded over his knee. Then came the agonisingly slow push of knee against knee. For a long-drawn-out minute she could not move, just abandoned herself to the sensation, to waves of heat and the promise of pleasure. The pressure increased meaningfully, hopefully, and Celia snapped her book shut, peeled off her glasses and stuffed them into her handbag. She rose, fighting for dignity and outward cool, and, tossing the man a quick glance of distaste, she walked away.

The image of his shabby, shifty-eyed appearance, his wet, drooping lower lip and greasy lantern-jaw, spcckled with blackheads, remained with her all the way home. She felt sick. In the bus, gusts of sickness alternated with panic. But she looked the essence of coolness and sophistication. She knew she looked calm because she had learned the trick at her yoga classes. Head up, as if it is hanging from the ceiling. Shoulders back and dropped down. Relaxed. Hands on lap, one resting, loosely curved, on top of the other, palms up. Like water lilies. Deep breathing from the back of the nose, breathe in, fill the chest and hold it. Breath out and relax.

Off the bus now and heels echoing along quiet streets. The crunch of gravel. The rasp of key turning in lock. The red-carpeted, centrally-heated luxuriousness enfolding her like a mink coat.

She closed her eyes and flopped against the door for a moment of exquisite safety before catapulting through to the sitting-room to pour herself a drink. Remembering just in time that Mrs Anderson from the villa next door would shortly be arriving for afternoon tea, she made it vodka instead of whisky and knocked it back neat. She was choking and coughing into her handkerchief when a blaring transistor heralded Wendy's return.

"Eh? Is this you tippling in the afternoon now, Mummy?"

"Wendy!"

"I'm only kidding! I'm only kidding!" Wendy rolled her eyes and went out again holding the transistor up to one ear and snapping her fingers. "Anything to eat?" she called back over her shoulder. "I'm starving!"

Celia followed her through to the kitchen.

"Don't touch any of these scones or cakes just now."

"Oh, Mummy!"

"Mrs Anderson's coming in for a cup of tea."

"Not Elspeth as well?"

"No, she'll be at her music lesson.But I don't know what

you've got against poor Elspeth these days. You used to be quite good friends."

"We used to play together. But that was ages ago when we were young."

Celia couldn't help smiling. "What's fifteen supposed to be?"

Wendy plucked a cake from the cake stand and stuffed it into her mouth before her mother could stop her.

"Legally I could get married," the words were chewed around with the cake, "in less than a year. So it's old enough, eh?"

"Don't speak with your mouth full. How many times have I to tell you? Is that the door?" Her face screwed up and her shoulders hunched, listening. "Surely that's not Mrs Anderson already? I haven't even had time to fill the kettle yet."

Wendy said cheerily, "I'll go."

Celia rearranged the cakes and put the stand on the trolley, but before she had the chance to do anything else, Wendy breezed into the room again.

"It was some silly twit collecting for Distressed Gentlewomen."

Celia's eyes widened with anxiety.

"What did you say?"

"No!"

"That was Mrs Holmes-Price!" Celia reached the outside door in time to halt Mrs Holmes-Price's offended flutter from the porch. "I'm so glad I've caught you. My daughter didn't realise who you were or that I was a regular contributor. Help for Distressed Gentlewomen is my favourite charity. I wouldn't like to think I'd missed doing my little bit for such a good cause."

A green felt hat that had been expensive fifteen years ago, when it had been purchased, was pulled well down over Mrs Holmes-Price's tufty grey hair. Its wide brim cast shadows over her pointed, twitching face. An orange-coloured scarf was knotted at her neck and she was wearing a shabby raincoat. She was cluttered with a notebook, a pencil, a crocheted handbag and a basket in which her pet chihuahua shivered despite his tartan coat and nest of blanket.

"My dear, you are always so kind. Dinky, say hello to kind Mrs King. Come now, be a good boy for Mummy. Say 'Hello, Mrs King.' Come now, for Mummy, darling."

The dog interrupted his shivers to give a quick sharp yelp.

"Isn't he cute!"

Celia cooed her appreciation and Mrs Holmes-Price managed to clutch the basket higher and made a sheaf of dry wrinkles with which to kiss the dog on the mouth.

"Mummy's clever boy, aren't you pet? He enjoys his little jaunts, you know, Mrs King." She peered, trembling with earnestness, from under the green hatbrim like a chihuahua herself. "He likes meeting people and saying hello. Don't you, Dinky, darling?"

"Of course he does." Celia paid over her usual contribution. "See you next month, Dinky. Goodbye, Mrs Holmes-Price. Thank you for calling."

Wendy was propping up the lintel of the kitchen door when Celia turned back into the hall.

"Mummy, honestly, what a pantomime. There just have to be better causes than that. Even you should know some."

With a sigh and a gentle push Celia managed to pass her.

"I do give to other charities, darling, but there's nothing wrong with this one."

"Distressed Gentlewomen!" Wendy hooted. "They've had it soft for too long. Let them fend for themselves. Let them rough it for a change. Millions never get a chance of any comfort. Never in their whole lives."

"Oh, Wendy, how can elderly ladies who've always led sheltered lives 'rough it'? They aren't used to roughing it."

"Well, it's high time they were."

"Don't be so unkind."

"They ought to think themselves jolly lucky they've had it so good for so long."

"Darling, be a good girl and take the trolley through to the sitting-room. Gently!" she cried as Wendy immediately swooped away with the trolley as if she were enjoying a ride on it. "Take your time or you'll have the cakes all over the carpet."

Left alone in the kitchen Celia tutted to herself. Wendy really was the limit. And her appearance was a constant source of embarrassment, too.

Why, oh, why did she never seem to want any pretty clothes? It didn't seem natural. Wendy's favourite, and indeed almost her only, articles of clothing were incredibly faded and patched jeans, tee shirts, a few sweaters, a denim jacket, and a duffle coat. She even went to parties in tattered denims.

And it wasn't as if she was a raving beauty and could afford not to care about clothes. She had frizzy red hair and freckles and she was small-boned and skinny.

The doorbell scattered Celia's thoughts and Wendy's answering bawl made her wince.

"I'll go, Mummy!"

Elspeth Anderson was so elegant and ladylike and she was only a few months older than Wendy.

"It's Mrs Anderson, Mummy!" Wendy's voice reverberated round the house again. Celia closed her eyes, took two or three deep breaths and fixed a smile on her face before going through.

Mrs Anderson was a fidgety woman with shrewd eyes.

"Mrs King, you look super as usual. I do envy you. You must be the happiest woman in Bearsden. My dear, fancy having a husband who has a beauty salon, of *all* things. You are lucky, aren't you? There's even his super partner to fuss over you as well." Her eyes narrowed. "I do love the Welsh, don't you?"

Mrs Anderson's scrutiny alerted Celia. Was there more to the question than appeared?

"Yes, they're wonderful people." She managed to speak sincerely. Owen, her husband's partner, was, as far as she was concerned, the only exception. She turned a smoothly pleasant face to her daughter. "Wendy, would you be a pet and bring the tea?"

"OK." She went away whistling.

"You seem to get everything you want, my dear. Not

just make-up and hair-dos." Mrs Anderson's eyes darted about. "I see you're wearing that suit you were admiring in Daly's the other afternoon."

Absently, Celia flicked an imaginary speck of dust from the skirt.

"I wish Wendy would take more of an interest in her appearance." Then suddenly pulling herself together, she gave a little laugh. "But she's a good girl and I adore her, of course. It's just an awkward phase she's going through."

Mrs Anderson's stare pierced and probed.

"Do you know what I think?"

Trying not to betray any uneasiness Celia raised a cool brow.

"What?"

"Wendy has a boyfriend!"

Chapter Two

It seemed strange to think that at one time nothing but flocks of sheep and the occasional horse and carriage used to pass Canniesburn Toll. A cottage still sat, marooned on a green pool of grass, between the roads but it did not look like the original toll house and as far as Joe knew, the manager of the Rio now lived in it. It struck him as an odd place to have a cinema. Cinemas were usually crushed between tenement houses and busy shops on main roads teeming with people; like Maryhill Road where he belonged.

The city of Glasgow dwindled away at his end of Maryhill. A large, tree-lined park helped to make the stretch of road that led to the separate Burgh of Bearsden a nowhere place, a no-man's-land.

The Rio Cinema crouched embarrassingly on the demure lace edge of the place that had once been part of Glasgow but had managed to detach itself from the common throng. The future held danger of reorganisation. The administrators in London threatened to allow Glasgow to engulf it, and, according to the local press, Bearsden meant to fight to the last man.

The present, however, was menaced only by rebels like Joe, who made defiant sorties to the Rio and even deeper into the middle-class fortress to bite like energetic fleas at the backsides of the inhabitants.

Police prowled the streets ever-ready to safeguard Bearsden's inviolability, but so far Joe had evaded them. He had infiltrated the Bearsden café at Hillfoot. He had acquired a Bearsden girlfriend. Wendy was fifteen, a year younger than himself, and she lived with her unsuspecting parents in the oldest and most prosperous part of the district known as "the village". There, the grey-stone villas had rolling lawns and tall trees and walls to separate and hide each family from its neighbours. Conveniently in the centre of "the village" was a boomerang of shops with the main Drymen Road curving into the road that led to Wendy's house.

Her hair was really something, nearly down to her waist and frizzy with waves. Her parents nagged her constantly about her hair; her father owned a big hairdressing salon on Great Western Road and he itched to get his hands on his daughter's head. She would not allow him to touch her and refused to go near his salon. Her mother kept wailing: "What will people think?" And her dad's favourite was: "One look at her, one look at that mess and they'll think I'm some damned hairstylist. She's enough to ruin my business."

They were always going on about what people might think. Instead of showing a bit of respect for Wendy, they did not even appreciate her figure. They called her skinny and said she looked like a walking mop. But Wendy was all right. Later he would be seeing her at the dance in the town hall. Right now he was heading for the café.

He tugged the hood of his duffle coat over his head, hunched beneath it, then stuffed his fists back into his pockets. Rain and wind were skittering and gusting and he did not want his hair to get blown about and ruined. He wondered if he would have time to wash his hair before the dance. If he did not stay too long in the café and shampooed it directly after tea it ought to be dry before he had to leave home again.

It was coming on great, his hair, down to his shoulders and longer at the back. He had it snipped short over his brow and temples to keep it back off his face because dandruff was one of the main enemies he had to contend with in the never-ending battle against pimples. Some of Joe's pals were one fiery red volcanic eruption and although they nicknamed him Beef because he was a bit on the hefty side, they envied his more or less clear skin.

Often he almost blurted out how he washed his hair nearly every day and experimented with all sorts of things from medicated shampoos to cider vinegar rinses for dandruff. He drank the cider vinegar for the pimples and his weight problem, too. You had to attack things from inside. You had to keep your bowels moving and flush yourself out with plenty of water and eat fruit and vegetables and cut out sweets and cakes or highly spiced stuff.

The only reason he hesitated to tip off the boys about all this was in case they thought he was going too far and getting soft. You could never be sure how things would turn on you. It was imperative to go along with the crowd. This afternoon, for instance, when he reached the café he would join the boys as usual in greasy, highly spiced hamburgers, or hambees as they called them, drowned in tomato sauce. They tasted great, but as he wolfed them, each mouthful became a pimple or a pound in his mind.

Then they would have snowballs. He drooled at the thought of his teeth sinking through coconut and chocolate, then squashing and sucking as tongue penetrated into thick marshmallow cream.

If there were chocolate Easter eggs they sometimes had competitions to see who could eat two the quickest. Gash Merrilees usually won. He could stuff two big eggs into his mouth at once while his cheeks bulged like footballs and chocolate juice dripped and spurted, his adam's apple jerking as the pieces went down.

Gash and the others belonged to Bearsden and they all (with the exception of Spiro MacLean who went to a fee-paying school in Great Western Road) attended Bearsden Academy. Joe was the only outsider because he came from Maryhill. Certainly it was the Bearsden end of Maryhill Road so it was near enough. Yet though the Drumchapel housing scheme was as near Bearsden on its other side, neither the Gunbraes, nor the Libby Dale boys, two of the biggest gangs from Drumchapel, were accepted by the Bearsden crowd.

He was the only Catholic as well. Celtic just needed to win a match for the café to explode with howls of "Catholic swine". They all dived on him and hauled him off his seat and pummeled him on the floor but it was good-humoured fun. Sometimes he laughed himself sick. He never needed to worry. Catholic or no—he was still one of them.

His musings suddenly disintegrated at the sight of trouble ahead. Three Gunbraes were approaching from the opposite direction but on the same side of the road. You could tell a Gunbrae a mile off. They had this special way of walking. Shoulders squeezed forward, head and chin capsized into neck and slightly twisted to one side, spine tipped back, fingers half in pockets, thumbs cocked outside, legs jerking, flicking feet.

Joe's nerves tightened warily. His mind raced like a hare with whippets after it as he weighed up the situation and assessed the best way to deal with it.

The Gunbraes were straddling the whole width of the pavement so he would either have to crush between them or step onto the road, giving them the pavement.

He rapidly came to the conclusion that the wisest and safest course would be the latter. If he walked through them, the chances were they would take it as provocation and jump him; if he crossed the road, they would take it that he was afraid—and jump him.

Concentrating completely—every movement, every expression had to be exactly right—he casually sauntered on through the rain, at the same time making sure he was near the outside of the pavement as he approached them. Then with poker face he stepped off when there was just a couple of feet between them. After he had splashed nonchalantly a few paces along the road and the Gunbraes had swaggered past without a word he returned to the pavement.

Before his fists had time to stretch out of their concrete stiffness, a white Zephyr with a blue police sign winking above it came crawling out of the misty rain. Two pairs of hostile eyes immediately hooked onto him.

He kept moving forward, not fast enough to look suspicious or afraid, not slow enough to look swaggering and impertinent. If he had been with the crowd maybe they all would have swaggered and laughed and fooled about as if they did not care a damn for the fuzz. But alone in the deserted street he stuck out, vulnerable, a target with no cover. They would have been gutter-hugging, watching the Gunbraes, but the Gunbraes would probably be in the Rio by now. He would suit their purpose just as well.

The car bounced forward in an eager spurt of speed then stopped suddenly, spraying muddy water over Joe's clothes. Resentment boiled up in him and he longed to pounce on the pair in the car and drag them out and squash their heads together, like a couple of cream snowballs. He could have, too. He was not called Big Beef McGouran for nothing. Sixteen years of life and experience had warned him, however, that violence was exactly what the fuzz were waiting for. They were just itching for an excuse to get him.

He kept on walking. Why, he asked himself bitterly, was everyone against you because you were young? There were two things that the Bearsden crowd, the Maryhill boys, the Drumchapel boys and all boys everywhere had in common—their youth and the fact that everybody older was against them. You would have thought that in the circumstances your parents would have lined up on your side, but no—they were the worst.

You were on your own—there was no doubt about it.

"Hey, you!" A stiff-capped head twisted out of the car window. "Come back here."

He would not have spoken to a dog in a voice that betrayed such open disgust. He could never understand it. What had he ever done, that's what he'd like to know? Why couldn't they act polite and say something like—"Could you spare a minute, sir?" or, "Excuse me, please, we would like a word with you"?

He stopped and turned round, his mouth twisting in silent sarcastic derision at the thought. Some hopes of that ever happening.

"Wipe that bloody stupid smirk off your pimply face for a start!"

He stared his hardest at them. They could not get him for just standing there staring. Or could they?

A pulse started to make jelly of his stomach. It wobbled through his veins and made him sweat. The cops were the whole older generation put together, were all authority, everything to be feared and hated and fought against. You had to defend yourself against the police and to do that was like trying to defend yourself against the whole world.

He boxed clever and said nothing.

"Where do you think you're going, fatty?"

"The café." His voice betrayed a slight tremble and he was bitterly ashamed of it. He hated the fuzz more than he had ever hated anything or anyone in his whole life.

"Well, watch it." The words were aimed with great accuracy. "Just watch it!"

The car splashed forward and Joe was flooded with relief. He mentally raised two fingers to the car before loping away.

The café was a great meeting place and it reminded him that not all the older generation were the same. The owners of the Hillfoot café were exceptions.

The old man, helped by his two daughters, served at the counter and his son Vince saw to the sitting-in part which was a separate room, with a door cutting it off from the shop.

They not only sold an incredible selection of sweets and

cigarettes, they also had quite a few tinned groceries and cakes and bread, and folk could always get the odd carton of milk if they were stuck and on Sundays they could buy most Sunday newspapers.

The thing the café was really famous for, though, was its ice-cream. Joe's mouth watered at the thought. The boys reckoned that Vince's ice-cream was the best in the whole of Glasgow. People came for miles around to queue up for it, especially on Sundays. On Sundays it was normal to see long rows of parked cars outside the café while their owners queued up for Vince's ice-cream.

Saturday was a busy day as well, but Joe ignored the queue of old miserable-looking housewives and balding bad-tempered men, pushed past them into the shop, grabbed the door-handle on the left and burst into the separate room.

It was funny. He felt more at home here than he did at home. This was his patch. The crowd lounging around were his crowd.

He trudged between the tables, still hunched inside the hood of his duffle. Spiro MacLean, so nicknamed because he was always putting his foot in it or getting someone's back up, jumped to his feet and began imitating and exaggerating his plodding walk and the high fatty bulk of his shoulder blades.

Joe knocked him aside with one hand and sent him sprawling on the floor amid a rattle of chairs. Hoots of laughter, including Spiro's, fought with yells of "Any money, Beef? Any cash? Come on, lend us a tanner for a cuppa tea."

Joe dumped himself at one of the tables.

"Get knotted! Hey, did three Gunbraes pass by not long ago?"

"Two wearing long khaki raincoats and one in denim jacket and trousers?"

"Aye."

"They came into the shop and bought some ciggies at the counter. The door was open and they glanced in here but when they saw they were outnumbered they thought better of it."

Joe guffawed and struggled out of his wet coat.

"They passed me down the road. I just glowered at them and they scuttled off. Then a bloody cop-car draws up alongside me and one of the fuzz—a right mean-looking devil with wee beady eyes, says, 'Where do you thing you're going?' So I says, 'None of your fucking business, mate.' "

Derisive yelps and throaty hoots and piercing whistles and cheers were accompanied by stamping feet, and he had to shout and gesticulate for peace and quiet so that Vince could hear his order for a Knickerbocker Glory. Thinking of ice-cream as he came up the road had given him a real craving for it.

"The guy's loaded," somebody gasped. "Lend us enough for a plain ice, Beef. Aw, go on, don't be so fucking mean."

"Get knotted!" Joe repeated automatically, then, in a more lively tone, "What's the latest about Thistle? Anybody heard?"

"Yeah!" Gash Merrilees answered. "The first eleven through the gate were picked for the team."

Joe gave a sarcastic, "Ha-ha!" and twisted round to watch impatiently for Vince and the ice-cream.

Somebody said, "Who's going to crash the ash?"

And one of the others plucked out a packet of cigarettes and passed them round. Matches rasped and soon smoke furled back and forth and thickened out in all directions.

Joe tucked into his Knickerbocker Glory with enthusiasm. He was glad he did not smoke. He had tried the odd cigarette when he was twelve or thirteen, but he had never really enjoyed it. Now he had more money for stuff he really enjoyed, like snowballs, and some to spare.

He was careful with money. He was not mean but he felt better with a bob or two tucked away. He had money hidden in his room at home and he had six pounds fifty in the Post Office.

"What about Thistle?" In between ice-cold fruity mouthfuls he tried again.

"One-nil."

"To Thistle?"

"Yeah!" Spiro bellowed. "But it should have been a goalless draw. The ref was biased."

Gash groaned. "For fuck's sake. It would have been at least three-nil if yon big Number Five hadn't kept fouling Johnny Gibson."

Joe wiped his lips with the back of his hand.

"Remember that time big Denis McQuade crossed the ball over from the corner of the pitch and Jimmy Bone flicked it on to Frankie Coulston and he first-timed it into the net?"

"Och, aye, not a bad goal, but the best I've seen was when Glavin passed a ball through to Jimmy Bone. Bone dribbled it round the keeper and side-footed it into the net."

"Well, that's them well on the way to the First Division." With great satisfaction and concentration Joe spooned the last of the ice-cream out of the tall glass. Yet as soon as the last drops were meticulously scraped and licked away he felt guilty and hated himself. That Knickerbocker Glory could be the cause of a whole new cluster of rotten pimples just in time for the dance.

"Who's getting the bevy tonight?" Spiro asked as if he did not know.

Joe glowered at him.

"How about you for a change?"

"For fuck's sake, Joe. I don't look eighteen."

"I never drink the stuff. It's got a stinkin' taste. I don't see why I've always to go. I don't look eighteen either."

"Yes, you do, you dope! And you're the biggest."

"But look at the size of Gash," he protested.

"His mouth, you mean?"

Gash made a grab at Spiro and knocked over Joe's glass. Joe dived to rescue the glass and juggled desperately with it, his face scarlet with laughter.

"OK, OK, I'll go, but it means meeting you lot before Wendy. Stop mucking about and hand over the cash. I haven't all night. I've my tea to get first."

They persuaded him to chip in despite the fact that he

would not be taking a share of the cheap wine he bought for them. They always preferred the wine to beer because it was more potent. They reckoned they could get drunk quicker on it.

Returning down the road to Maryhill he whistled cheerily to himself. It felt good to belong to such a group. Things had been very dicey when he was younger, before he met Wendy and before he found the way to Bearsden.

He remembered how the Maryhill boys used to jeer and catcall as he walked down the road. It was a relief when he reached the dark tunnel of his own close but even there they followed him with their stone-throwing and their taunts. That was how he developed his self-conscious, huddled gait. You could not stop and fight all the time. Anyway he was ashamed of what his dad was and on that score his heart was never in a fight.

From the time the Maryhill boys found out about his father he had no friends at all.

Now he lived in secret dread that the Bearsden crowd would get to know.

As usual he suppressed the fear of discovery and of losing the trust and respect of his friends and his place in life way back into the most inaccessible part of his mind. He locked the door on it. He did not know what else to do.

Thinking of his father made his cheery whistle wither and die in his throat.

Now he forced the town-hall dance to fill his mind with pleasant pictures. He heard the volume of the music batter against the walls and bewilder the ear-drums. He saw Wendy sway and shake in tune to the beat.

He licked his lips and found his whistle again and the sound defied the rainswept Maryhill Road and his father.

Chapter Three

"Wendy!"

Celia fondled the banister of the stairway as she called her daughter. The hall glowed with polished rosewood which reflected the opulent warmth of the red Turkish carpet and the ruby lampshades.

"I'm in the bath!"

A quick little sigh of annoyance disturbed the smoothness of her make-up like the sudden rippling of a pond.

It was never any use depending on Wendy for anything. The child seemed to have developed a positive talent for causing not only inconvenience, as in this case, but, on too many other occasions, downright embarrassment and trouble.

Tension screwed up Celia's shoulders, locked the muscles at the back of her neck and made a washboard of her brow. Her eyes closed to concentrate on her yoga breathing and she cupped her hands in front of her waist, palms up, fingers relaxed in the "water lily" position. Gradually she relaxed.

Mrs Anderson had stayed rather later than usual and now there was not much time left to prepare dinner. If she wanted ice-cream for the *coupe-jacques* she would just have to go down to the café for it herself.

She checked an impulse to call up to Wendy that she was going out for ten minutes. This shouting habit of Wendy's was becoming infectious. One of these days she would find herself shouting like a fishwife when some of her friends were in. She shivered at the thought but her feet gained comfort from the thick carpet as she climbed the stairs. It was not a big house compared with some of the others in the immediate vicinity but it was a good solid villa.

It was as if Wendy knew that she was approaching the bathroom door to give it a discreet tap and bend her black coiffure towards it and smile and say gently, "I'm going out for an errand, darling. I won't be long."

A transistor radio started blaring before she reached the landing.

Water splashed in competition and Wendy's voice bawled out.

"Oh, honey—honey, da—ra—da—da . . . oh, honey—honey . . ."

"Wendy!" Her knock was quick and panicky. "People will hear you outside!"

"Da—ra—da—da . . . oh, honey—honey!"

"Wendy, the neighbours!"

Grabbing the handle of the door she rattled it vigorously. Then suddenly the door opened under her hands and Wendy stood naked, dripping water all over the bathroom floor.

"I might have been anybody," Celia gasped.

"Eh?" The naked figure shook and shuffled from one foot to the other in tune with the music. "Da—ra—da—da . . . oh, honey—honey!"

"Don't be disgusting!"

"Eh?" Wendy looked straight at her for the first time.

"Get your dressing-gown on."

"Why? I'm not finished yet. Mummy, you are awful. I can't even get peace to have my bath."

Long spindly legs clambered back into the water, buttocks and body thin and undeveloped like a young boy's.

The bathroom was in a shocking mess, water and clothes and shoes and the contents of a handbag spilled all over the floor and the radio in the midst of it all blaring defiantly.

Celia felt a balloon of rage blow up to bursting point inside her head but she managed to ignore it and speak quietly.

"I'm going down to the café. We're having *coupe-jacques* for sweet."

Wendy splashed round and her youth made Celia wince. A blue satin ribbon tied in a bow on top of her head held up most of her hair but clusters of red-gold tendrils and curls drooped down and her freckled face was an open book of childish curiosity.

"Why don't you call it ice-cream?"

"The proper name of the sweet we are having for dinner is *coupe-jacques*."

"But it's just ice-cream."

"Hurry up and get out of that bath. And get this dreadful mess cleared up. It's a disgrace. A big girl like you. What if someone came in?"

She closed the door, her heart thumping. The walk to the café now seemed a welcome escape, a chance to breathe deeply, to draw in what the yoga teacher called *Prana*, the calming refreshing life-force.

Wendy did not realise how lucky she was. She had no reason to be critical. If she had had the same kind of parents as her mother! Never to her dying day would Celia understand her parents' cruelty towards her. Her unexpected arrival on the scene when they were middle-aged, bordering on elderly, had no doubt been an embarrassment, but surely such a phenomenon had happened to other couples, especially childless ones, and delighted them.

There could be no getting away from the fact, however, that her parents were shocked and bitterly ashamed and had never forgiven her for being born.

Their hatred was always there, a hidden claw with long talons eagerly awaiting the chance to draw blood. It only needed a few impulsive skipping steps, as she walked between them on the way to church, to incite a hissed warning that if she did not behave herself they would perch her on top of the pulpit in front of the minister and the congregation and everyone would see what a wicked girl she was.

At other times the threat was that a van with a loudspeaker on top would career round Bearsden bawling out all the stupid ridiculous things she had done. She lived in constant fear of rejection and ridicule. Yet at the same time a childish trust, strengthened by a hope that was never quite crushed, kept pushing her towards the waiting talons.

As a child she was never prepared, she never learned by experience.

Wendy should benefit by it, though. She had tried to redress the balance and be extra loving and patient with her daughter. She made a point of encouraging her in every way she could.

For example, Wendy said she wanted to go to art college when she left school. Her father, on the other hand, had set his heart on getting her into the salon to train as a hairdresser.

He kept protesting angrily.

"I'm worried sick about the shortage of staff all the time. The least she could do is come into the salon and give me a hand."

She always tried her best to please Peter but on this issue she defied him.

"It's her life. We mustn't ruin her chance of fulfilment and happiness."

"She's likely to be far more 'fulfilled', as you so quaintly put it, if she comes into the salon. Hairdressing's creative. I'm as good an artist as any that comes out of the art school. And I make money at it!"

She could see Peter's point of view and, in actual fact, she would far rather see Wendy safely installed under her father's wing in the salon.

Who knew what kind of place the art school might be and what kind of strangers she might get mixed up with? There would be people from all over the place, not just from Bearsden.

Thoughts of Wendy being launched into a world of wild drinking, drug-taking and immoral students filled her with fear and panic. The child was so innocent and vulnerable. She could not bear to see her hurt. Perhaps she should try and persuade her tactfully that it would be better to go in with her father.

Anxiety furrowed her brow and she turned into Milngavie Road and the café automatically, not noticing where she was going. The man at the counter jerked her back to her immediate surroundings.

"Yes?"

"Oh . . . A large tub of ice-cream, please."

A door opposite the counter opened to a burst of deep-throated laughter and a crowd of large gawky youths came crowding out. As soon as they saw her they acquired a sheepish air and became subdued and silent.

Then one of them managed to say, in passing, "Good evening, Mrs King."

The others gave self-conscious smiles.

She recognised them as Wendy's classmates from the Academy and she knew most of their parents. They were all comfortably-off business or professional people.

One day these young men would be settled in safe respectable lives as doctors and lawyers and businessmen. As the wife of one of them Wendy could have a respected place in the community and no one could point a finger at her. But there was plenty of time. Wendy was a worry but she was still only a child. There surely could be no question of boyfriends just now. She wondered all the same if she ought to question Wendy. Mrs Anderson had somehow made her feel uneasy and there was no telling what ridiculous thing Wendy might do next.

The tub of ice-cream froze her curved palm as she returned home.

Often she nearly succumbed to the temptation of pleading with Wendy never to do anything that might make anyone gossip or "point the finger of derision and scorn" as her parents would have put it.

"Oh, please don't . . . oh, please . . ."

Her shoulders went taut with embarrassment and she cringed at the thought of the ridiculous Victorian overtones of such a scene and how it would make Wendy giggle.

One could not bare one's soul like that now. One was not a child any more. One just went on living, skating gracefully along the icy surface of life, calmly, confidently, willing oneself never to think about falling.

It was just a worrying stage Wendy was going through. Everything was perfectly all right.

The street lights picked her out in the doorway, a small figure conservatively but elegantly dressed, with a stiff, slightly hunched posture as if she were continuously sensing danger.

"Hello, Mummy." Wendy came strolling down the stairs with her transistor held close to her ear. "Daddy's in."

"Set the table, darling. I didn't realise how late it was."

"OK. Will dinner be long? I'm starving."

"I've just to dish it."

"Owen's there as well."

"Oh?" Her hesitation was a tiny bridge that needed effort to climb across. "That's nice."

Owen would be moving in with them again if she wasn't careful. Hardly a day passed now without Owen being in the house. During the summer Peter had been too busy to take a holiday and had persuaded her to have a couple of weeks without him. He promised faithfully to come for the day on Sunday when the salon was closed. He came all right but Owen came too. And she discovered that Owen had been staying in the house during her absence.

She put her head round the sitting-room door and smiled at her husband's partner.

"Will you be staying for dinner, Owen?"

"Of course he's staying," Peter said.

The smile stuck to Celia's face as she retreated.

The latest pop group were yelling their heads off in the kitchen. She made no objection for some time but eventually murmured:

"Darling, dinner's ready. Would you mind switching that off now?"

"Sure!"

"I'll pass the plates through."

"OK."

Wendy went whistling away to the dining-room then suddenly her head and shoulders burst through the hatch.

"The Studds are coming to the town hall."

Carefully Celia dished out the casserole steak.

"I worry about you going to dances."

"They're fab."

"It's not the dances, dear. I've no doubt they have very nice dances in Bearsden. But you're only fifteen."

"Fifteen's grown-up nowadays, Mummy."

"Is that them all?" She strained up on tiptoe to peer

into the dining-room. "Tell Daddy and Owen to come through."

"Daddy! Owen!"

"Wendy, stop bawling like that. It's a dreadful habit and so unladylike."

Wendy groaned and rolled her eyes.

"It doesn't help to make silly faces," Celia said as she peeled off her apron and left the kitchen.

The men were approaching from the sitting-room side of the hall. She entered the dining-room in front of them, amazed at how different they looked, Owen hefty and dark haired, Peter fair and slim.

"You sit over there, Owen."

"Anything you say, girl."

Smoothing her napkin neatly over her knees Celia smiled across at Wendy.

"Are you going with one of the girls in your class, darling?"

Wendy's freckled cheeks bulged with food. She shook her head, then after swallowing over a couple of mouthfuls managed.

"No, Big Beef."

"Big Beef?"

"His nickname. His real name's Joe."

"Do I know him? What does his father do?"

"No, he's from Me-e-ryhill!" Wendy imitated the coarse vowels and rolling r's of the broad Glasgow accent. "He's a fitter—whatever that is. I don't think Joe's sure about his dad himself. He goes all cagey when you mention him." A beam of interest snapped into life behind her eyes. "Maybe he's a spy or a crook. Maybe he's doing time just now in Barlinnie!"

"Wendy!"

"You haven't put any bread on the table," Peter announced in an aggrieved tone. "You know Owen likes bread."

"What? I thought I . . ." She felt confused and taken aback.

"It's all right, girl." Owen's face creased into one of its dimpled smiles and he rose.

She rose too.

"No, I'll get it, Owen."

"I should know my way around the kitchen."

"I'll get it."

"Sit down, Celia," Peter remonstrated.

She dwindled into her chair.

Chapter Four

Peter had not made love to her for months and she couldn't pluck up enough courage to speak to him about it.

She wanted to ask: "What's wrong? What's wrong with me, for God's sake?"

She prayed that he would tell her.

Often she rehearsed exactly what she would say when he arrived home from the salon. But he frequently worked late and as the hours of waiting dragged past she would need to keep bolstering up her courage with a drink.

"Peter, please, all you have to do is tell me that I'm doing something wrong. I'll try my best to change . . ."

"Peter, we can't go on like this. I know everything seems wonderful on the surface. We have a lovely home. I have lots of beautiful clothes. You're very generous. But, darling, oh, please . . ."

Then one night he had arrived very late with Owen. She had been more than a little drunk and Peter had insisted that she sit and talk to Owen while he prepared supper.

"Well, Owen . . ." She found herself gazing coyly at him over the rim of her whisky glass. "Make yourself at home. Help yourself . . ." she giggled and flopped back in her chair, "to a drink."

It occurred to her that he wasn't bad looking. If you liked dark-eyed heavily-built men. He looked like an Irish navvy, curly black hair, dimples and all. Or a gypsy. Only he wasn't Irish—he was Welsh.

She allowed her frothy négligé to slither back to reveal her legs, neat and shiny and pink like a doll's.

To her delight, he flushed and she swayed from the chair towards him. She was thinking what a marvellous sensation it was to disturb a man, to make him aware of one's femininity, to fire his blood with the craving to possess it.

Her smile was tender although her eyes were glazed. She looked at his handsome face but through an invisible mirror saw her own features melting towards him.

"Let me help you." Her smile erupted into a husky little gurgle. "I'm good at pouring out drinks. I'm good. I'm very good."

The longing to be taken hold of nearly overwhelmed her as she reached the sideboard and the whisky bottle. She was so near to him that she felt the heat from his body. A pulse began to throb in her and she thought that he must surely know how she ached for a man, any man.

He just stood, not saying anything, not doing anything except avoiding her eyes.

The whisky bottle swayed over his glass before clinking roughly against it and splashing the golden fluid. She replenished her own glass next, took a gulp from it then peered up at him with a mixture of anger and desperation. "What's wrong with you, eh? Cat got your tongue? Don't just stand there!"

Peter swooped into the room pushing the trolley in front of him. The thick carpet muffled the sound of the wheels but the cups clinked loudly.

"I've made some sandwiches, Celia," he said. "You'll be all right after you've had a sandwich and a cup of tea. Then off to bed with you!"

"To my own little bed."

"To your own little bed."

"In my own little room."

"In your own little room."

He kept glancing over her head at Owen. She felt frightened.

"Peter."

She pushed her head against his chest and clung to his waist.

"Come with me."

There was a little pause and although this time she could not see, she knew he was looking at the other man.

"Right now?"

"Yes."

"All right. Come on."

Going up the stairs with his arm encircling her waist she tried to pretend that it was the same as when they were first married. Life was warm and exciting, full of love and promise. Yet as the bedroom opened up towards her she saw only a nightmare of hopelessness.

In a way she felt like laughing.

It was a beautiful bedroom. She had made it beautiful, even more beautiful and inviting than the rest of the house. She had made it a feminine froth of a room. Frilled curtains looped across the window and a light white fourposter bed was an enticing confection of frilly drapes. White furniture was enriched with fine gold filigree and on the floor the soft curly pile of the carpet added to the warmth and comfort. Yet she felt cold and afraid.

"Peter, stay with me. Come to bed."

Gently but firmly he disentangled himself from her arms.

"Owen's waiting," he said.

"To hell with Owen, Peter, forget about Owen. Come to bed."

He folded back the bedclothes and she untied her négligé and dropped it on to the floor. He picked it up, folded it neatly and draped it over a chair.

"In you go," he said brightly.

She could see the pinks mounds of her breasts, with their milk-chocolate tips, wobble like a blancmange under her nightdress as she clambered between the sheets.

"That's the way." He tucked her in. "You'll be all right now. What you need is a good night's sleep. See you in the morning."

There was an eager speed about his long legs as they made for the door. She watched them with blurred eyes.

The door shut quietly. She was alone with her reflection in the mirror opposite. A not unattractive woman, a woman who did not look her age, a petite well-shaped woman with flawless skin and black hair and large brown eyes.

She felt confused. She did not believe she was beautiful; to her, beauty meant being tall and blue-eyed and blonde. Yet she could not persuade herself that she was *ugly*. Surely she was at least as attractive and desirable as any other normal married woman?

Maybe it was something that she could not see. Maybe it was something in her nature, or some habit she had that repelled Peter and he was too kind to speak to her about it. She would plead with him to tell her. "I want to know," she'd say. "It's me, isn't it? There's something wrong with me."

She struggled out of bed and into her négligé. Satin ribbons slithered away under fumbling fingers. Defeated by them she left the garment hanging loose and, forgetting about slippers, wove a zig-zag path from the room, her toes curling into the carpet.

As she descended the stairs leaning heavily on the banisters she heard sounds of male laughter. The sitting-room door was open. It was an Aladdin's cave of comfort. The lamps gave a warm red glow. Curtains and cushions glistened. The clock on the mantelpiece whispered persistently under its glass dome, its gold balls gently rotating.

Then Owen came into view. He was staggering and swaying as if he were drunk. He was ogling Peter and saying in mock-husky sexy tones:

"Let me help you. I'm good at pouring out drinks. I'm good. I'm very good!"

Peter was laughing.

Celia shrank back and, still clinging to the banisters, returned upstairs. She lay in bed, heart thumping, mattress and bed vibrating.

Loyalty, it always seemed to her, was the first essential of any marriage. Her parents had been loyal to each other.

Their bond of loyalty had been so strong it had shut her out. Watching from outside the little private world they alone shared, she had envied them. One day, she thought, I'll be loved and safe like that.

It had seemed like a dream come true, yet at the same time a hundred per cent safe and sensible, to marry Peter. They had been married quickly and by special licence during the war. Peter had only been seventeen and in the RAF and she had just been a child out of school. But they both belonged to Bearsden and had known each other all their lives.

There had been a brief happy time before Peter had to return to his base. Not long after that he had been shot down over Germany. She had not seen him again for years and nothing had ever been the same after that because over there he had met poor, handsome, hard-done-by, clever-clever, dear dimpled Owen.

Chapter Five

Joe's father, Aloysius McGouran, took pride in knowing about the place where he belonged. He knew, for instance, that in a contract dated 1793 a woman called Mary Hill granted "feu of that ground laid out for building a town upon, which is to extend from Glasgow to Garscube Bridge . . . and to which it is hereby provided shall be in all times called the town of Maryhill".

Many a brutal attack had taken place in Maryhill in the days when there were no street lamps and no policemen. It was very risky to walk along the Maryhill Road then. The "cowardly, lounging and slinking ruffians", as they were called, had a favourite meeting place at the top of Kelvin Street. From there, passers-by would be showered with stones and half-bricks or whatever else came to hand.

The hours of darkness became so dangerous, in fact, that the inhabitants presented a petition to the Sheriff of

Lanarkshire pleading for the place to be made into a police burgh.

But Maryhill had long ago become part of Glasgow. During the day Maryhill Road was as busy with traffic and pedestrians as Sauchiehall Street. There were long queues of buses and heavy lorries, but instead of the smartly-dressed office-workers and Sauchiehall Street shoppers, there were swarms of dirty-faced men in dungarees and women swathed in headscarves.

Darkness made a backcloth to the road now. It was quieter. Long stretches of pavement lay empty in front of black-windowed shops. But street corners were littered with swaying, disputatious men who had been disgorged by the pubs. Chip shops blazed with yellow light and, like moths, shadowy figures drifted towards them.

McGouran stopped the car outside one of them and bought a fish supper and two pickled onions.

A mouth-watering smell titillated the warm air inside the car as a few minutes later he swung into Seldon Street. He felt a sag of disappointment at the emptiness of the place. Further along, at Celtic Street, there would be men hanging around the Ram's Head, laughing and arguing and talking. But here in the short cul-de-sac next to the Church of the Immaculate Conception there was only one close.

A building loomed up in the shadows across the street, but like so many old tenements in the Maryhill Road area, it was empty and in ruins. In grey rotting stone, windows, like dead men's eyes, were black hollows of desolation. Closemouths gaped as refuse and rats swelled inside and old newspapers crept sadly along the pavements.

The red sandstone building on his side was good for a few years yet, though.

He flicked another hopeful glance around as he locked the car.

The hot grease of the fish supper oiled his palm. There would have been plenty of chips to share with someone. In his imagination, the lobby rumbled with male laughter and talk as he entered the house and switched on all the lights and opened cans of beer and said: "Come on, lads, make yourselves at home. Draw a seat up to the fire."

Only there was no one there. The house, like the street, was silent. The fire was out. A flimsy nylon stocking caught at his size eleven shoes. His wife's knickers, underskirt, crumpled dress, all the clothes she had discarded when changing, were strewn across the kitchen floor.

She would still be at the bingo and God alone knew where Joe was.

Disappointment hardened into bitterness.

He had just come from his father's house. He had made the old man a cup of cocoa fired with the usual tot of whisky and helped him to get settled safely into bed.

A fat lot Joe would ever do for him in his old age. That was part of the trouble with young folk nowadays, they were bone selfish. The other thing at the root of all that was wrong with the likes of Joe was lack of discipline. There was nothing to equal the discipline of the Church, and Joe was not getting that.

It had been a different story in Aloysius McGouran's young day.

The Catholic schools were the last to give up the tawse and their punishments were always twice as severe as those delivered to any erring children in the nearby Protestant schools.

Religious discipline and high standards had affected every aspect of his life. Often his mother used to say, "Don't you ever do anything in this house that Our Lady would be ashamed of!"

He had been taught his prayers from the moment he could talk. He had learned to identify each holy picture and statue.

At primary school the diligent teaching of prayers had continued and he had learned the Catechism. Then, as well as the three "Rs", there were religious examinations to prepare for the sacraments of Penance and Holy Communion.

He had tried his best to make sure that all the children God had blessed him with received the benefit of the same

Christian background and, of the five alive, four were good Catholics. Joe was his only failure.

Joe had taken the sacraments of Holy Communion and Penance when he was twelve and that was it. He had hardly ever set foot in the church since.

Yet to hear Joe talk at times anyone would think he was the sinner. Of course he had never been forgiven for the time when, in his capacity as magistrate, he had sentenced some of Joe's pals to a spell in Borstal.

"Look, Joe," he told him at the time, "you step out of line and behave like a young hooligan and I'll have you flung in the nick. Don't think being my son will save you."

Joe had given one of his infuriating hoots of laughter. Infuriating, because it strained at the edges with bitterness and sarcasm and self-pity.

What had Joe to be bitter or sorry for himself about?

He came from a good home. He had been given a fine education and soon he would be going to art college. His mother was against the idea of Joe going to college just as she had been against him staying on at school but he had firmly overruled Biddy and Joe was getting his chance.

Was Joe grateful, though? Not on your life!

McGouran kicked Biddy's clothes aside and then noticed one of the brown and yellow striped towels that he kept in his drawer to be used only by himself.

She had been in his drawer again. Rapid strides propelled him from the kitchen, across the lobby and into the bedroom. There, sure enough, the drawer in the bottom of the wardrobe lay open and some of his clean clothes spewed out.

Fury shot to the top of his head like a rocket and battered at his brains.

As if it were not bad enough that the slut never mended or ironed his clothes, she would not even give him the chance to take decent care of them. She could not care less if he appeared at council meetings in the City Chambers or on the bench looking like a tramp. She liked to dress to kill when she went to her bingo, though.

He ached to kill her. His fingers longed to fasten round

her fat white throat and strangle the stupid useless life from her body.

Fury frittered down to palpitating weakness and he sank down on one of the single beds and sat with his head cupped in his square spades of hands.

He wanted her. He hated her. For years now, ever since the twins, of which Joe was the only survivor, were born, Biddy had refused to sleep with him. That birth had been bad and there had been a hell of a long time between Dave and the twins—seventeen years in fact. The twins had come as a shock. He understood that. But, Holy Mother of God, Joe was nearly seventeen now and Biddy over fifty. She surely could not imagine there was any danger of another pregnancy.

He needed her. He despised everything about her from peroxide blonde head to fat feet bulging from high-heeled shoes. Any woman could have filled his needs better.

Any woman would have been more acceptable to him.

He heard her come in then. Her key scraped slowly, furtively, and her heels met the floor with caution.

He shot out from the bedroom and confronted her. She gave a squeal of fright.

"Jesus! Oh, it's you! I thought you'd be in bed."

"You've been in my drawer again. You've used my towel."

She jabbed him aside and bobbed into the kitchen like a balloon pinched in the middle.

"So what?"

He followed close behind, his neck projecting his head forward aggressively.

"Leave my things alone."

"Look at the fire. A fat lot of good you are."

"I've been down the road seeing to the old man while you've been enjoying yourself at the bingo."

Biddy kicked off her shoes, lit a cigarette, then sat down and cocked one foot up on top of her knee so that she could massage her toes. Her skirt strained and rucked up revealing pink bulges of flesh at the top of her stockings and an orange nylon mountain at her groin.

"Why shouldn't I enjoy myself at the bingo? I work bloody hard for any pleasure I get. As it happens, I've been next door to see to Teresa before coming in here. You're not the only one who does good works."

"If you touch my drawer again, I'll kill you!"

Biddy peeled the cigarette from her lips so that she could laugh.

"Your drawers, did you say?"

He took a step forward, his eyes protruding, his hands held out stiffly, like two bunches of bananas.

"I'll kill you!"

A noise from the lobby stopped him in his tracks. It sounded like Joe. Yet the heavy tread was uneven and jerky, a drunk man's stagger.

McGouran swivelled his attention towards the door.

"Joe?" His anger kept in tight rein at first, then suddenly escaped and racketed through the house.

"Joe!"

Chapter Six

The town hall looked and sounded like hell's kitchen. Psychedelic lights rotated on each side of the stage sending flames of colour writhing up the wall behind the group. Other beams of colour stained the group, making one side of their faces green and the other red.

The floor of the hall alternated between complete blackness and a black and white fast flicker that made the dancers look like actors in a jerky silent film without the silence.

Four huge amplifiers on the stage dwarfed the group and continuously bombed the place with ear-exploding sound. The booming pandemonium was too loud to be contained and blasted though the walls and roof, bombarding the whole of Bearsden.

The door into the hall was at the side of the stage and when Joe and Wendy entered they had to walk past and round a curved line of Drumchapel boys to get to the opposite side, where they usually sat in between dances.

Some of the Gunbraes were skinheads and had their hair shaved to tufty bristles that made them look younger than their sixteen or seventeen years. They wore crumpled shirts with the sleeves rolled neatly above their elbows, braces hoisting their very tight denim trousers, and large workmanlike hobnailed boots.

Others sported Fair Isle pullovers and hand-made shirts and clumpy round-toed shoes with fashionable red or yellow laces.

Joe trudged past them with Wendy at his side. He was wearing the trousers of his brown suit. He had taken the jacket off and left it in the cloakroom so that he could show off his fitted, green, short-sleeved, button-down-collar shirt.

Wendy nudged him before they sat down so that he would turn his face towards her and see what she said.

"There's an awful lot of Gunbraes here tonight." Her mouth exaggerated the shape of the words but she did not attempt the impossible task of competing with the noise from the amplifiers.

Joe shrugged as if he could not care less.

Wendy thought he was the best looking boy in the place.

While he made nonchalant whistling shapes with his lips and at the same time eyed the Gunbraes, she took stock of him.

She liked his Roman nose and strong jaw-line. There was something Roman-looking about his hair, too, the way it was cut short across his brow and swept down long at the back.

He fished a packet of gum from his pocket and flicked a piece in her direction.

She said, "Ta." And they both began chewing energetically.

Her bright green stare switched to the group of girls dancing in front of the stage.

They were all spiky. That is, they all wore tight jerseys and leather or velvet chokers and midi skirts just below the knee. Their shoes were high at the front and had high, thick heavy heels. Some had hair straight back in a bun. Others had theirs cut short on top and some long strands left here and there. Feathered, that style was called. Only a few maxi skirts could be seen.

Wendy happily tapped her foot to the rhythm and enjoyed a look at the bouncers standing guard at every side and at each corner. They were ancient, about forty—but tough. One looked like a giant with a broken nose. Another was just as broad-shouldered but smaller with tiny black-currant eyes and long arms, like an ape.

She became aware of Joe prodding her and immediately turned, smiling towards him.

"Would you like to dance?" he mouthed with great care.

She nodded and they strolled on to the floor and began the spine-swaying, undulating ritual; elbows clamped to sides in a posture that was the same as the Gunbraes'.

The singer was now adding to the clamour.

Noise resounded inside Wendy's head. Her brain seemed to rattle around like hard peas in a metal pail.

Thought became impossible. Wonderful. Noise engulfed even the innermost secret places; blanked out the hydrogen bomb, her parents, death, the unknown, all terrors, all anxieties. The world was hypnotised, bewildered away.

Vaguely her eyes saw the twitching, flickering forms growing and multiplying and crowding all around.

The Gunbraes stamped their feet.

"Gunbrae! Gunbrae! Gunbrae! Gunbrae!"

Then like a slap in the face, the music stopped. She wandered, still dazed, back to where she and Joe had been sitting.

She turned to speak to him and was taken aback. He was not there. Suddenly, she felt vulnerable and afraid.

"Joe?"

Her face became a white button in a frizzy red mop. The Gunbraes had caught Joe in a menacing circle and were pummelling him, pushing him about.

In a flurry of outstretched hands, she chopped a way through a crowd of girls towards the circle but halted when she saw Joe's big fist shoot out and up and lift one of the Gunbraes into the air by the chin.

She giggled hysterically. None of Joe's Bearsden pals were here yet to help him. They would be drinking their bevy under the Scout Hall. But Joe was worth ten of them anyway.

He had lost his temper. She could see by his flushed face and the reckless way he lashed out in all directions.

Now the bouncers were wading in and the Gunbraes were having to fight them.

Yells, screams, oaths, bawls, thumps, cracks, clatters, arms, legs, feet, heads, and blood hotchpotched on the floor. Every now and again a bouncer erupted, clutching a Gunbrae by the collar and ran him swiftly out of the door. Until there was only Joe left. And the group exploded into sound again and no one paid any more attention.

Wendy helped Joe to his feet and they both examined his clothes to see what damage had been done.

His trousers were all right, apart from some dust which they meticulously brushed off. But one side of his green shirt was torn where one of the Gunbraes had booted him.

Wendy squeezed his arm and mouthed up at his face, blotchy now and wide-eyed with anxiety. They both knew what torn clothes meant to parents. A hole in a shirt meant more to parents than a hole in the head.

"Don't worry, I'll sew it."

He looked at the tear and fingered it and looked at her again.

"It'll be all right," she assured him. "I'll do it tonight."

They were playing a slow tune now and Joe grabbed her and they shuffled from side to side in time to the music.

He was nonchalantly chewing gum again and not even looking at her. She felt the heat of his big hands clamped on either side of her waist and was happy. She gave herself up to amplifiers and the flickering lights and one dance after the other and all the time being with Joe.

It was sad when the noisy night emptied away and the group packed their gear into the waiting van outside and queues for the cloakrooms dwindled and the ordinary ceiling lights went on and everything looked shabby.

But she still had Joe.

They strolled hand in hand along Drymen Road and turned the corner at the shops, laughing and talking.

Then suddenly they heard a roar of voices and a clanging of feet rampaging towards them.

Wendy felt Joe give the slightest twitch before stiffening and standing his ground. She felt the momentary urge to run too but quickly decided that if Joe was brave enough to stay she must be brave too.

They did not say anything, just remained hand in hand watching the mob, dressed in long tattered khaki raincoats, come howling towards them.

They went down like ninepins and Joe was kicked away from her and rolled, like a ball, screwed up, knees to chest, arms protecting head.

She scrambled to her feet and wildly lashed out with her handbag. Sobbing and crying, she made blind rushes at the crowd aroundJoe, using her body as a battering ram.

Suddenly the sound of a car dispersed the mob like magic.

"What's going on here?"

A man's head eased out of the car window as she struggled to help Joe up.

"For goodness' sake, George," a woman's voice urged from inside. "He's just another of those long-haired louts."

The dark night sucked the car away.

"Come on, Joe," Wendy sobbed. "I'll take you to my house and get you cleaned up before you go home."

There was blood pouring down his face and shirt and trousers and his jacket was ripped and hanging half off.

He groaned and retched as if he were going to be sick.

"Look at my jacket, Wendy." His words mumbled from a stiff swollen mouth. "They'll kill me at home!"

"Oh, Joe!"

She tried to piece the jacket together, to hold it up, to see what she could do but it was beyond her and she wept with frustration.

Her handkerchief was too small to stem or mop up the flow of blood and she could not find his.

"We'll be all right in a minute," she tried to console him. "We're nearly there."

Their feet crunched on the gravel as she led him through the darkness round the back of the house and into the kitchen.

She turned on the cold water tap and made him bend over the sink while she gently wiped him with a wet towel.

Already his eyes were puffed up and discoloured and she could see where most of the blood was coming from. A deep laceration on his forehead kept welling up and spilling over, reddening his hair and face.

"Oh, Joe," she kept saying, and then her mother called from the sitting-room.

"Is that you, Wendy?"

"Here's a cup of water, Joe. Drink it while I go and tell Mum."

As soon as she entered the sitting-room her mother's expression changed from a gentle gaze of enquiry to stark horror.

"Wendy! There's blood on your clothes." She rose, spilling her knitting from her knee in a flurry of panic. "What have you been doing?"

"Oh, my God!" Her father looked away. He could not stand the sight of blood.

"It's not mine," Wendy gasped with impatience. "It's Joe's. He's through in the kitchen. Oh, Mummy, please come quickly. I think he's hurt bad. He was in a terrible fight."

Her mother's eyes protruded.

"Get him out of here!"

Wendy stared in silence for a minute, not understanding.

"Get him out of here!" her mother repeated in a desperate hiss. "At once!"

"He's hurt."

"He's a hooligan."

"I told you she was mixing with a bad crowd," Peter groaned, still averting his face from her direction.

"You're not going to help Joe?"

She spoke half to herself, her voice high and childish with incredulity.

Then she looked hard at them both and said:

"I'll never forgive you. Never as long as I live. You're a couple of bloody hypocrites. All you two are good for is hiding your heads in the sand."

Chapter Seven

Peter had looked so handsome in his RAF uniform. Celia had been the envy of all the girls in Bearsden. She wondered why he had singled her out from the others. Every girl in her class was crazy about him, and that was not surprising. The well-cut uniform had flattered his slim figure and matched the blue of his eyes.

There had been years, of course, when those eyes had barely glanced in her direction. At ten he had courted a little girl called Joanna. She remembered him at the primary school waiting for Joanna's class to come out so that he could walk home with her. Some of the other boys had taunted and tormented him for keeping company with a girl so much and he had fought them to teach them a lesson.

All through school he had to fight for one reason or another. In each new class he had to fight the biggest boy and beat him to prove himself and prevent himself from being bullied.

After Joanna, who eventually moved with her parents to another town, there had been Dorothy, then Jean, then Peggy.

It was not until he was in the RAF that he suddenly turned to Celia. Outside of school they had often met in the café, at church, at the tennis club, at scout dances, but they had always been with a crowd of friends.

Now he singled her out. They went alone to the pictures in town or to a restaurant and he told her about how he was training to be a pilot and soon he would be moving further south to another base. From there he expected he would be flying on raids over Germany.

They talked a lot. Or rather he talked. She was happy to listen, yet sad and frightened at the thought of him going far away and into danger. An urgency developed about their relationship, a conviction that everything had to be accomplished, organised, settled before he went away.

Everywhere young couples were rushing into marriage for the same reason.

They obtained a special licence and waited a long time in a queue of couples at the registry office, but the marriage ceremony itself only took a few minutes.

Looking back she was sure they had been happy then, although at times Peter had seemed strangely withdrawn. Sometimes even when she was lying in his arms she had the feeling that he had wandered far away from her. "Penny for them," she had asked and he just answered, "The war."

This she had understood. They had been as happy as they could expect in the circumstances. Then he had gone away. She remembered him at the railway station immaculate in his officer's cap and gloves, brusque and cheerful.

"Be seeing you soon," he had promised.

The next she had heard from him was via the Red Cross from a prisoner-of-war camp in Germany. His first letter told of how he had been shot down and captured. It said not to worry. He was all right. The place was not the Ritz. The overcrowding had to be seen to be believed and he had experienced some difficulty in adjusting to this; as an only child he had been used to a room of his own all his life, and silence at night.

But the German guards at the camp were not too bad and the Red Cross made life bearable. They got Red Cross parcels, for instance, and often, helped by a bit of bartering, the guards would supply other requirements.

Subsequent letters gave instances of this.

A theatrical group had been formed and he was one of the actors. The guards had at different times managed to supply the group with materials with which to make costumes and other odds and ends for props.

Gradually the camp theatre featured more and more in his letters. They had no female entertainers, of course, so some of the group had allowed their hair to grow long in order to play women's parts. He had been persuaded to go along with this. Many a good laugh they had while practising talking and walking like women and they had become quite expert at making up their faces. The theatre, in fact, was a godsend. They would have gone mad in that place, he said, if they had not managed to have something.

"You would not believe your eyes if you saw me now," he wrote. "My hair is far longer and more glamorous than all the others'. It's right down over my shoulders. Some of the other chaps don't look nearly so realistic because their hair is coarse and bushy. Mine is fine and straight.

"Remember my white silk scarf? Well, I rub my hair with it every night and morning, polish it like mad. You've no idea how shiny and glossy it makes it. That's a good tip for you, Celia!"

He began experimenting with other hair aids like rinses and conditioners. Make-up and beauty tips began filling his letters too.

"If you can't get make-up, Celia—I know things are in short supply at home too—there are lots of ways to improvise. We have had to do this for the group. We started out with not one lipstick or dab of mascara between us but you should see the wizard cosmetic kits we have now.

"Our wardrobe isn't too bad either. We each have a long evening dress of sorts. Nothing really glamorous, you needn't feel jealous! I have quite a nice skirt and blouse. I had to shave my legs but mine weren't so bad as some. Some of the other chaps' legs were revolting—all black and bristly. It's amazing how smooth and white they were underneath though. They looked quite attractive eventually. I swear to you, Celia, we could fool you or anyone when we are all dressed up. No one could possibly tell that we are men."

She did not know what to think of his letters. She had

grown up with a picture of him in her mind, an intense knowledge of him as a person on which her whole future existence was built. But her picture and the picture the letters painted bore no resemblance to each other. Every month another letter arrived to increase her confusion.

"Celia, I'm so excited. You'll never guess! The chaps have voted me the best hair and make-up artiste as well as actress. From now on they want me to style their hair for them and help them with their make-up. Honestly, Celia, I'm really quite good. I seem to have a flair. I was thinking I might take it up after the war. No, not might. I will! One day I'll have my own salon. I'm so excited. I'm just thrilled to the core.

"They are a wizard bunch of chaps, our lot. Living in such close proximity can have its strains and tensions, you know. Some of the prisoners squabble and become generally nasty. Others let themselves go and are equally nasty. There's nothing like that with our crowd. We help each other. We are loyal to each other. We think the world of each other. We live harmoniously together.

"There are some really good chaps here, Celia. Good Christians. There's Owen, for instance. He always wears a little gold chain with a crucifix on it round his neck. He is a very good-looking man too, though some of the chaps think he's a bit moody, but they don't know him as I do. Owen confides in me.

"Poor Owen has had a lousy childhood. His father is a proper bastard and his mother sounds a bit of a weakling. She never seems to have been very successful in standing up for Owen against the old man when he was small. He says she tried. That is when he talks about his mother at all. Most of the time he just keeps telling me what a bastard his father is. Owen has never had a chance. He has never known what happiness is."

She began to dread the letters. They seemed to be hurtling Peter further and further away on some disastrous journey over which neither of them had any control. She wanted to do something, anything to bring him back to her and to his old, familiar Bearsden self. But the whole grotesque twisted world of war was against her. From the sentimental slush of—"There'll be bluebirds over the white cliffs of Dover . . ." to the blasphemous—"Praise the Lord and pass the ammunition . . ."

Nobody was sane any more. All the old moralities, including truth, had gone. In the context of war there was nothing anyone could do to help her or Peter.

"Darling," she wrote to him, not knowing what to write. "Please try to remember what it was like before. Remember peacetime in Bearsden. Remember the trees in the streets and the gardens. Remember how you used to play football in the park. Remember your friends. Remember me . . ."

Then she burned all the letters about the theatre group, and Owen. As if she were terrified that someone might see them.

Chapter Eight

"Did anyone see you?" Celia had asked Wendy. "Did anyone see you come in with the boy? Did anyone see the fight? Were there police? Was anyone there?"

Wendy's mouth twisted and there was contempt in her eyes.

"Don't worry, Mummy. Not one of your precious Bearsden ladies witnessed me letting you down. You can have your turn of the coffee morning with a perfectly peaceful mind."

"Don't be impertinent, Wendy," she had murmured automatically. Her mind was in chaos. She felt exquisitely relieved. No one knew.

Yet, once she was sure the danger from Wendy's friend was past, she began to worry about him and feel ashamed.

He was only a young lad, still at school.

She tried to convey regret through the twisted barbed wire of her anxiety.

"Your friend's all right now, isn't he? He did get home

safely, didn't he? I was so shocked and surprised when you came in, you see—you were all covered in blood, Wendy. I . . . really . . . I got such a shock. I just didn't know what to do. I hardly knew what I was saying."

Wendy just stared, green eyes cool chips of marble.

"Wendy, I wish you knew how I feel. I wish you could understand."

"I understand. You're ashamed of me. You wish I was like Elspeth Anderson. Keeping up with the Joneses or the Andersons is all that matters to you and Daddy."

"No, no, dear. You mean everything to me. You're . . . you're . . ."

"An embarrassment. I don't fit the Bearsden pattern like Elspeth. The grown-up pattern, that is."

Peter came in then.

"You can't be half as embarrassing to your mother as you are to me. Look at that hair! It's pathetic. If I wasn't a hair stylist and you weren't my daughter—I'd laugh!"

Wendy's voice acquired a tremble.

"Elspeth Anderson is the perpetuation of the older generation and all they stand for."

"Hooray for her! We'd all sleep more peacefully in our beds if you were like Elspeth."

Suddenly Wendy's face crumpled with bewilderment.

"I can't understand why you like her so much. She's so selfish and she talks about nothing except money. That's her yardstick for judging everything and everyone. Appearances and material things and money, money, money!"

"What's wrong with money?" Peter demanded, but Wendy continued as if she had not heard him.

"Yet, it's the like of her who condemns everyone else. You're the same. You just hate anyone on sick benefit or the dole."

"Elspeth's father and I work hard for our money. Why should we be forced to carry no-users on our backs? Why should we help to pay to encourage loafers and layabouts to expect something for nothing?"

"If there's any allowances or grants going, you'll see that

you get your share, or more if you can manage it, and there's all the business and tax fiddles, aren't there?"

"Now, Wendy," Celia cautioned. "That's quite enough. I won't have you being impertinent to your father."

She believed that it was for Wendy's good that the status quo should be maintained. A child must have security, and discipline of the proper kind was one form of security.

A father must be head of the house and merit and receive respect. He was, after all, the provider, the breadwinner. the security of all of them rested in his hands.

He was the pillar on whom their home, their display window to the world, their accepted and acceptable pattern of life, depended.

His voice increased in intensity but not in volume. Sometimes Celia thought the only thing she and Peter had in common was this acute awareness and concern about what people might hear or see or think.

"You've picked up some scruff from Maryhill and now you've decided to go all bolshy, is that it? Is this what we've to suffer now? I suppose Bearsden's become a dirty word, like money. Well, money buys you plenty, m'lady, and you ought to think yourself damned lucky you've been brought up in such pleasant and comfortable surroundings among decent respectable people."

"Mrs Anderson tells Elspeth not to bother about love but to marry a man with money."

"The best of luck to her!"

"Money's so important to Elspeth she gets quite excited and boasts about it when she manages to sneak off buses without paying her fare."

Peter laughed and made a face.

"So she saves a bob or two."

"Why can't you and Mummy ever speak the truth? Stealing's stealing, not saving!"

Peter whirled on Celia.

"Would you look who's standing there judging us all?" He flung an arm in Wendy's direction. "Wouldn't it get on your wick? She looks like something the cat dragged in. She picks some Ned from Maryhill for a boyfriend. She goes to these unspeakable dances. She gets involved in street fights. And then she talks as if there's something wrong with us." He shook his head and scratched his neatly trimmed side-boxers. "I don't know!"

"I know you don't know." Wendy burst into tears and rushed noisily away shouting, "You and Mummy don't know anything!"

Afterwards, hovering outside the child's bedroom in an agony of uncertainty, listening to the brokenhearted sobbing, Celia wished Wendy would just be content to enjoy life in a harmless fashion like Elspeth. Life was so much easier that way. Life's problems were reduced to finding a pretty dress or resisting an extra cream cake, or keeping to the sunniest spot in the garden in order to acquire a good tan.

She often thought of Elspeth and longed for the peace of mind that having a daughter like that would bring. And all the time Wendy remained in her mind's eye; the pale, caring face and uncared for appearance; the look of intensity, the terrifying honesty. Yet she knew Wendy was a better person than Elspeth. She secretly admired her daughter's courage and felt bitterly ashamed of her own cowardice.

Celia always cringed inside when she remembered one particular incident when Wendy was quite small. She had often remarked to the child how dreadful the atom bomb was and had indicated sympathy with protestors after reading about a "ban the bomb" demonstration reported in the papers at the time.

Then one day she had been appalled to discover that Wendy had organised some of her little friends in a sit-down demonstration at Bearsden Cross. In a flurry of acute embarrassment (it was a Saturday of all days and the place was seething with people), she had grabbed the child and rushed her home, leaving the placard crudely printed with the words—"Ban the Bomb—Jesus Would Not Like It!"—lying crumpled in the gutter.

Afterwards she had tried to justify her action without condemning the child's.

"It's not that you were doing anything wrong, dear. I mean, I admire what you were doing. It's just that Mummy was afraid for you getting into trouble. The police might have thought you were being naughty taking up room on the pavement like that. They might have tried to move you and I couldn't bear the thought of you being upset."

She knew it was a feeble excuse and she suspected that Wendy knew too.

Now she was aware of her own callousness towards Joe. The boy might have been dying and Wendy was the only one who had compassion and courage enough to help him. Her pain was in the realisation that if the incident were repeated, even if the boy were dying—her reaction would be exactly the same.

Sometimes her love for Wendy contorted into hatred. It was not fair that the child should torment her so. She wished time would speed up so that Wendy would be away to college, or married, or emigrated to some far-off land. Anywhere, anything. She wanted the child to be happy, of course, but surely she was entitled to a little peace of mind herself.

Why should she not enjoy a placid existence gossiping and drinking coffee and eating home-baked cakes with her friends? Why should she not spend her life sunning herself in her pleasant sheltered garden? Why should she not enjoy filling her time with pleasant diversions, the Ladies' Guild, the tennis club, the bridge club, yoga, squash, and nice films like *The Sound of Music?*

Why should she not feel, like her friends, that those who did anything different with their time like voluntary social work were "do-gooders", and "odd"?

She tried to rally patience to her aid.

It would all pass. She knew children had difficult phases; perhaps Wendy would not be rebellious for ever.

She stood calmly, with her hands cupped in the water-lily pose, and smiled at her daughter.

"I'm sure Joe's a very nice boy. One must never judge a person by the district he comes from or how much money he has or the accent with which he speaks. It's what's in the heart that matters."

"Yes, Mummy," Wendy said.

"The only criterion, the only yardstick for judging anything or anyone should be—does it or he or she hurt anyone else."

"Yes Mummy."

"It's true, dear. It really is."

"I know it is Mummy."

She patted the child's fiery, frizzy head.

"You're a good, kind girl."

But touching her daughter did not seem to bring her any closer. She fondled the hair then smoothed her fingers over the freckled cheek.

"I know you would never mean to hurt or worry anyone." Her gaze wandered. "But you must see that it's natural for Daddy and me to worry about you and the type of people you mix with. You might have been the one who got hurt."

"Yes, Mummy."

Her fingers retreated from the velvet skin.

"It's time for my yoga practice now."

She was wearing black stretch slacks and a black sweater and looked nearly as slim and supple as her daughter. The only difference was the slight forward slope of her shoulders as if they had set that way after a lifetime of supplication.

Gracefully she sank down, cross-legged, on the floor. A little gentle wriggle now to make sure she was in the proper position. Shoulders eased back, head up, tummy in, knees out wide, down, down. Relax . . . relax . . .

"Don't worry, dear, you'll meet lots of other nice boys after you leave school and go to college."

Calm . . . calm . . . there could not . . . there must not be any more trouble.

Smile serenely . . . close eyes . . . completely blot everything out.

Chapter Nine

The letters kept coming. No flames could consume them. Nothing could ever blot them out.

"Celia, what a giggle! Owen and I escaped. Yes, actually got clean away from the camp and into the town. They picked us up after a few hours and here we are back again. But honestly, it was a giggle while it lasted!

"There we were, walking along that German street bold as brass, me dressed in a skirt and blouse with a headscarf tied over my hair and mincing along in high-heeled shoes. You should have seen my make-up, too. It was really beautiful. Owen said I looked a real doll. You know how fair and fine-textured my skin is, and I only needed to use a very little face-powder.

"No one would have guessed. I mean, there we were strolling along as if we owned the place and me hanging on to Owen's arm as if I were his best girl.

"It was Owen the soldiers recognised eventually. They still didn't tumble to me and were going to cart him off on his own. Honestly, Celia, I'm not just having you on. I'm sure I could have got away with it.

"But when it came to the pinch I just couldn't leave him. It didn't seem right. I saw the way he looked at me as they were about to haul him away. He has very dark brown eyes, so dark that sometimes the black of his pupils seems to creep over and swamp the brown. On that occasion his eyes were completely black and anguished and appealing. I just couldn't let him down.

"So here we are, as I say . . ."

She knew all about Owen. Gradually, piece by piece, he became an intimate reality to her.

He smoked a lot and often in the middle of the night he had spasms of coughing. Peter worried about this and he would lie listening in the dark to the rhythmic sawing of Owen's breathing. When the breathing suddenly tripped, jerked, then stuttered into coughing, he leapt up to fetch Owen a drink of water or a sweet to suck. Peter saved sweets from his Red Cross parcels especially for this purpose.

Owen came from Wales and had a rich sing-song accent. Owen was taller than Peter, who was thin with long bony hands and straight finely-textured hair. Owen was more muscular. Owen had springy black curls. Owen wore a crucifix round his neck and on his wrist an identity disc glistened on a fine silver chain. Owen had deep dimples. Owen was a lovely singer. Owen had a tiny cluster of warts on the back of his right hand and two fingers and the thumb of the same hand were chocolate brown with nicotine stains. Owen's toe-nails were thick and hard and square and they were fiendishly difficult to cut.

Owen had suffered a dreadful childhood. His father had never ever addressed one civil word to him. A dreadful, sneering, churlish brute his father was. "What a life, Celia," Peter wrote. "Imagine being brought up in that atmosphere.

"And of course Owen comes from a very poor working-class home. We've been very lucky never knowing any place but Bearsden. Bearsden is pretty cushy, you must admit. It must sound like seventh heaven to Owen. He keeps asking me about it. I have to laugh. He must know every nook and cranny of the place by now and everything about everybody in it. What a man!

"I told him. I said, 'I can see you ending up in Bearsden yourself yet, Owen.' Immediately his eyes lit up and he said: 'Is that an invitation?'

"I believe he really would come to Bearsden, you know."

She wondered what Peter meant. She wondered what Owen meant. Was Owen thinking in terms of not just coming to Bearsden but actually coming to their house?

She addressed questions to a mind tightly locked in self-defence against answers she did not want to hear.

In her letters of reply to Peter she tried to divert him away from his apparent obsession with his friend. She asked him about himself, about his health, about his plans for the future. She told him she loved him and pleaded with him to write and tell her that he loved her too. She told him all the news about Bearsden and Glasgow and about their mutual friends.

She realised that he was only allowed a limited number of letters and obviously there were difficulties in keeping up any related correspondence. She also appreciated the fact that he was living an unnaturally confined and concentrated existence and it wasn't surprising that life back home had lost its reality. But she kept assuring herself that after the war, after he was home again everything would smooth itself out and be perfectly all right.

Poor Peter. She hoped that this awful Owen person was not taking advantage of his friendship.

Peter had always been such a sensitive and kindly person and his intense concern for his friend was really rather pathetic.

In one of her more light-hearted teasing-type letters she had said: "Good gracious, darling, you do go on and on about your precious Owen, don't you. You almost seem to love him like a brother . . ."

Back had come the indignant reply.

"Of course I love Owen! Why shouldn't I?"

Then came the build-up of plans for the future.

". . . We've made up our minds, Celia. Owen and I are going into partnership after we get out of this lot. We're going to pool our money and buy a hairdressing and beauty salon. We'll take a training first, of course. We'll work and study like Trojans and when we get our own place we'll employ the best people. We plan to have a really high-class salon. I thought I'd eventually try for something in the Great Western Road area. There's bound to be premises going there at some time. We have so many plans, Owen and I . . ."

She struggled to cope with her anger. She tried to feel glad that instead of Peter suffering and getting depressed and ill as many POWs did, he had found companionship and something with which to occupy his mind.

Why not a salon? Peter had an artistic temperament and might do very well in this profession.

Why not Owen? What was wrong with having Owen as a business partner?

After all, Peter was no fool. He had come from a business

family. Surely he knew what he was about. Anyway the whole idea might evaporate once the war was over and the men were free.

Owen would fly back home to Wales where he belonged. And Peter would happily, eagerly, return to her.

But Peter wrote:

"Oh Celia, I'm heartbroken—poor Owen! His mother has died. He'll never see her again. Now he has nothing to look forward to, nothing to go home for. I've never seen the poor soul so frightfully depressed. 'The Jerries might as well finish me off here and now,' he says. 'Nonsense,' I told him. 'You've everything to live for. You and I are going to have a happy and rewarding partnership.' I nursed him along the best I could but at times he had me really worried. Honestly, I thought for a while he might even commit suicide. 'Think of me,' I kept telling him. 'Think of me.'

"He's a good chap really, but he can be difficult. A couple of times a fight flared up between him and some of the other fellows. I managed to smooth things over but not before one of the men got a broken nose and another lost half his teeth.

" 'What am I going to do with you, Owen,' I scolded him. 'You're an awful man!'

"Then suddenly he couldn't help laughing. In fact we both had a good laugh and it was such a delight to see that awful heavy cloud of depression lift from him again . . ."

To rid herself of her own monstrous cloud she joined the Red Cross and slaved night and day nursing military personnel. In many ways she was happier at this time than at any other in her life. She liked men and the fact that she was sent to work in military hospitals and camps, where she was constantly surrounded by them, exposed all her nerve ends and tuned them precisely into pleasure.

It was a secret joy to arrive in the ward each morning, her butterfly cap a crisp white contrast to her black hair and the long soft sweep of her eyelashes; her belt drawing admiring attention to her tiny waist and the provocative bulge of bust and hip.

She laughed at the wolf-whistles at the same time as scolding the men. Often she had to plead for silence in case Matron heard them when, for instance, they greeted her with an enthusiastic rendering of, "If you were the only girl in the world, and I were the only boy . . ."

Many of them pestered her for dates, and she smiled and said: "I'm sorry, I'd love to but . . ." Proudly she flashed her rings. "I'm afraid my husband wouldn't!"

Their attention lit up the dark places of her mind even if it were only a temporary and artificial brightness.

"What would my husband say to all this?" she protested in mock indignation. Or, "It's a jolly good job my husband can't hear you." Or, "Is my husband jealous? Of course my husband's jealous . . ."

She had written to Peter and told him about the way the men flattered her and tried to make dates. She had even exaggerated a little. Then afterwards she had felt guilty and had nearly worried herself sick while waiting for his reaction.

When his letter of reply came she pounced on it and immediately tore it open praying that he had not been hurt or worried or jealous.

". . . I only wish Owen was there . . ." he wrote. "It sounds such a jolly place and such a nice friendly crowd. Obviously they are happy and well cared for and that's what Owen needs. He looks as hard as nails but I'm sure Owen is developing bronchitis and needs hospital treatment. If only he were safely away from this awful place and in one of those neat white beds in that lovely sunny ward you described.

"But as a next best thing, could you please, please try and help us by proxy, Celia. Advise me, tell me what I should do, tell me what I ought to give Owen for his awful cough."

It had taken her all her energy to control the urge to write back one bitter word in reply—

"Arsenic!"

Chapter Ten

Joe was glad it was Sunday and he did not need to get up early for school. Gingerly he eased himself over on his back. Every part of him throbbed and ached with pain and it was an effort of will to open his swollen eyes. Through slits he gazed at his painted sketches of Snoopy and Linus and Charlie Brown round the walls of his room.

All the time he listened.

The house seemed quiet. He reckoned it might be safe to get up. The chances were that his mother and father were at Mass. They were both proud of the fact that they were good Catholics. His mind sought ways of dodging them, of getting out of their road before they returned.

He dreaded another bedlam like the night before.

His father had nearly gone mad.

"Look at the good suit that I paid twenty pounds for!" he roared.

His mother pushed his father out of the way.

"Glory be to God! Come into the kitchen, son."

Joe winced as she slapped a wet cloth over his face while his father tugged incredulously at the torn pieces of jacket.

"I work hard to earn enough money to keep clothes on his back and look what he does. Look all he cares!"

Biddy pushed Joe's head down over the sink and spoke over his humped shoulders.

"Oh, shut up! Anybody would think to hear you talk that you were the only man who ever worked."

"All the time I'm trying to keep things decent . . ."

"Holy Saint, Al!"

"And it's hard enough with you behaving like a slut without him starting to act like a hooligan."

"May our blessed Lady forgive you for calling me a slut. I'm as good as you any day and don't you forget it. Just because you did a bit of skivvying for the union and they gave you a leg onto the council . . ."

"Don't show your ignorance in front of the boy. I was voted into the council by Glasgow ratepayers at a free election. And I was made a bailie by my colleagues on the council."

Biddy's laughter was bitter.

"And you enjoy that, don't you? Sitting up there on the bench kidding yourself you're God Almighty. Nobody's been good enough for you for years. Everybody's ignorant. Everybody's sluts!"

"Not everybody—just you! You know your trouble, Biddy—you're jealous. You're jealous of my good reputation in this town. You're jealous of what I've made of my life."

Pain began to spin around in Joe's head and he cried out and jerked away from them.

"You're always the same. Both of you. You're never any use."

"A fat lot of use you are," his father roared indignantly. "Look at you! You're a disgrace. You ought to be ashamed. What sort of company have you got yourself mixed up with? Where have you been?"

"Bearsden."

His mother hooted and lit a cigarette.

"Bearsden! What a scream! He gets all sorts of la-de-da ideas from you. Maryhill's not good enough for him for one. And he wants to stay on at school for another. So instead of getting a job and making a man of himself and putting decent money in his pocket and giving me a pound or two for his keep, I've to go out to work while he loafs about the streets getting himself into trouble. The Bearsden streets, no less. I thought your Bearsden pals were 'spanking blokes', son."

"I was with my girlfriend and it wasn't our fault . . ."

"Oo!" Biddy widened her eyes as if she were impressed. "Womanising already, is it?" She took a quick puff at her cigarette. "Were you fighting to protect her honour or relieve her of it, son?"

"She can't be much of a girl," his father said, "if this is the sort of trouble she gets you involved in."

"It wasn't her fault, I told you. It was the Gunbraes."

His mother bristled.

"That's a Proddy gang, isn't it?"

Joe wiped his mouth very carefully with the back of his hand. His lips felt as if they were going to split and burst wide open. It was agony to move them to form words.

"Yes," he mumbled, not bothering to add that it would not have made the slightest difference if they had been the Libby Dale boys. Anyway it was more the street a boy came from that determined the gang he was in, not so much religion. He had heard that there were at least two or three Proddy boys in the Libby Dale.

His father's craggy face twisted in disgust.

"Gunbraes. Proddy Gang. They're only a crowd of stupid wee boys who haven't yet grown up. They've neither self-discipline nor parental discipline, nor discipline of the Church. Nor have they been instructed in better ways to employ their energies and time. I thought you had more intelligence, Joe. I really thought you had more intelligence. You like painting and drawing, don't you? You want to go to the art school, don't you?"

"Yes."

"Well, Holy Mother of God, what do you think you're playing at? You might have been run in by the police. You might have had your life and your career ruined before it even started."

Biddy hung her cigarette from the corner of her mouth and screwed her eyes against the drifting smoke as she began to put in her rollers. The rollers, straining her hair back, revealed dry, grey roots under the glossy blonde and made her face larger and rounder. She was not unattractive in a plump, bouncing way, but something always spoiled her appearance; a pair of cheap dangling earrings, a girdle that was too tight, shoes with too low fronts and too high heels.

Now she said, "Oh, shut up! Did Proddies never have a go at you when you were young?"

Joe longed for the comfort of bed. He felt sick and near to tears.

"You don't understand. Religion doesn't matter."

"What?" His mother's hand stuck with a roller in

mid-air over her head. "In Glasgow? You must be joking, son. Here . . ." Her voice changed as if something had just occurred to her. "This girl—she's not a Proddy is she?"

"I don't care," Joe said brokenly.

"She is!" His mother swung round on his father. "You're the clever dick who encouraged him to hang around Bearsden. He'll be telling us next he wants to get married. See you!" She turned to Joe again. "Your granny'll kill you. There's never been a Proddy in our family."

"He's only sixteen and he just said she was a friend, you fool. We've all got Protestant friends, haven't we?"

"Don't you call me names. I warned you. And this is all your fault. I told you you'd be the ruination of that boy. He would have been happy and settled in a decent job by now. Or learning a decent trade if you'd let him. But, oh, no, you've to try and make him into an artist. An artist of all things! What kind of money do you think he'll ever make at that?"

"Art was his idea, not mine. I'd rather see him going in for a man's job like engineering any day . . ."

Joe did not wait to hear any more. He stumbled away to his room and fought back his tears as he undressed and crawled into bed. But the salty moisture welled up and nipped down his face despite his efforts and he burrowed under the blankets and prayed that no one would come and witness his shame.

Now he eased himself up and padded across the room on his bare feet to open the curtain.

Every Sunday his gran came over to have her Sunday lunch and spend the afternoon with them.

If his mother told her about Wendy (and she would) he would never hear the end of it. Gran nagged at him enough about not going to church. According to her he was destined for hell and damnation, nothing surer.

He decided to go early to the café and have a hambee there for lunch and maybe do some sketching to pass the time until the rest of the crowd came. They usually met there some time on a Sunday afternoon.

He had a wash and bathed his eyes, took a couple of

aspirins with a cup of tea and felt much better. He still looked terrible, though, and he knew that his pals would be angry at what the Gunbraes had done to him. They would insist on reprisals and revenge.

He thought of the inevitable return fight with mixed feelings. It was good to have friends who cared what happened to you and were willing to wade into a rammy on your behalf. At the same time he felt sick to his soul and wished that it were not necessary.

All he wanted was a peaceful life; a few laughs with his pals in the café, a game of football, a pass in English, history and art in the "Highers", a good enough portfolio to get him into art school and the occasional date with Wendy.

Yet he knew the necessity, the inevitability of the reprisal fight.

The Bearsden boys would have to show the Drumchapel boys that they could not come into their territory and attack one of their friends.

As sure as night would follow day, next Saturday at the Bearsden town hall he and a crowd of Bearsden boys would congregate.

The Gunbraes would be only too well aware of the procedure resulting from their attack of the previous week and they would be at the dance in force. There would be forty or fifty of them.

The police would be there, too.

Already in his mind's eye Joe could see the flashing blue lights of the police-cars and hear the howling of their sirens.

His stomach caved in. He would give anything to avoid the whole thing. Yet to chicken out was unthinkable. Impossible to go on living after such a cowardly act.

No, he had to fight side by side with his pals. And he would fight. And he would think himself lucky to have such pals.

There was trouble ahead and the knowledge saddened him but there seemed nothing he could do. It was part of his life and the only way to meet it, as far as he could see, was head on.

Chapter Eleven

The policeman called:

"Case number eighty-five. Bring in John Doyle."

Another policeman opened a door and echoed his voice down a long corridor.

"John Doyle!"

McGouran slowly rustled through some papers before peering up. He sat above everybody else in an inset part of the room, like a stage, on which only the top half of him was visible. With his Roman nose and beady, belligerent eyes, he looked like a hefty Punch deprived of his Judy.

The charge was droned out by a bored official.

"You are charged with urinating . . ."

McGouran growled down at the youth:

"Guilty or not guilty?"

It was always the same on a Monday morning, especially after a Saturday football match. It was as if the police had cast a net and dredged in every long-haired, pale-faced, grubby, cheap, crumple-suited horror in the City of Glasgow and far beyond, then trickled them out, one by one, in front of him.

"Guilty, your honour."

"Have you anything to say for yourself?"

The youth shifted uncomfortably yet with an air of resentful impertinence.

"Well, me and my pals came all the way up in the bus from Greenock and . . . and, eh . . ."

McGouran loudly interrupted him.

"You'll have to arrange for your buses to stop at toilets and not disgorge yourself and piddle all over our town. You're fined ten pounds."

The official murmured: "Do you wish time to pay?"

"Yes, sir."

"I have no objection, your honour."

"Thirty days to pay," McGouran said.

And the policeman signalled the youth to leave.

". . . bring in Andrew Bell."

"You are charged with breach of the peace . . ."

"You have three previous convictions." McGouran thumbed through his papers. "Is that correct?"

"Yes."

"Well, have you anything to say about this?"

"I would be glad if you could give me a chance, sir. If you could see your way."

McGouran stared at the shabbily-dressed man standing before him for a long silent time. At last he said:

"Well, what am I supposed to do with you?"

"If you could give me a chance, sir. If you could see your way."

"What kind of chance can I give you? What have you learned from your internment?"

That was the trouble, he thought. They never learned anything. Back they all came time and time again, until he knew their names and their faces and their silly excuses and their promises off by heart; the old winos, the young hooligans, the thieves, the wife-beaters. And nearly every offence that arrived before him had been committed under the influence of drink. It was enough to put any decent man off his pint.

"You're one of these drunken pests who're always causing trouble at these matches. You're fined forty pounds!"

A small, fat woman in a large floral headscarf bounced immediately to her feet at the back of the room and cried out:

"Oh, my God!"

A policeman took an aggressive step towards her and gesticulated authoritatively.

"Sit down!"

Like a punctured balloon she puttered back into her seat.

McGouran knew what forty pounds meant. He would have been hard put to it to rustle up such a large sum himself. Yet what else could he do? He had lost all faith in prison sentences doing anything except toughen or embitter a man. Or if a first stretch and a normally decent person were involved it sometimes killed him.

Dode McPhee was a typical example. He was an ex-bailie

he had known and respected for years, a man who had devoted a lifetime to helping other folk. The reason why Dode succumbed to bribery was still a mystery. He died a broken man within a month of coming out of prison.

No doubt the fact that councillors were not paid had a lot to do with the tragedy. A great many expenses were incurred in local government work, and maybe it was all right if you were a businessman and always had a pound or two to spare in the bank. If you were an ordinary working chap, though, the dice were loaded against you at every turn.

Some employers were not at all keen on giving you time off during the day to attend to council business. Even if they did, you were not usually one of their favourite employees and your chances of being picked for promotion were practically nil.

"He's hardly ever here," was the attitude. "Give it to the other guy."

So you never got any extra money and your expenses and worries mounted up. In the course of council business you met famous people and dignitaries from other countries and even members of the Royal Family. To mix with people like that you obviously had to keep up appearances. That meant good clothes and the ability to buy someone a decent meal or return a drink they had stood you.

Of course the businessman's grouse was that he could not claim. He did not get compensated for loss of earnings when he took time off his business.

The Scottish Nationalist candidates maintained that there was a real flaw in democracy as far as they were concerned. They said the Tory businessman was his own boss and the Labour man was usually a union official and was therefore backed and protected by the union. But the SNP candidate was out there on his own, and already three had been sacked from their work because thay had to take time off for council business.

There was nothing democratic about that, they insisted.

It was another argument in favour of councillors being paid, he felt.

Some of McGouran's Labour friends, like Bert Flynn, worked constant nightshifts to make a bit of extra money. That way he could attend all the meetings at the city Chambers in his own time too.

He was flogging himself to do it though. He was bound to be tired and at a disadvantage compared with a prosperous businessman who was refreshed and mentally alert after a good night's sleep.

Men like Bert Flynn had to be really dedicated. It was not as if anyone appreciated what you did. People usually viewed anyone in politics with the deepest suspicion.

Now McGouran glowered suspiciously down at a curly-headed, blue-eyed man with shoulders like an ox. He was dressed in a khaki combat jacket, open-necked shirt, denims and heavy working boots. A handsome Irish navvy any woman could have been forgiven for marrying.

McGouran remembered the case.

"Am I to understand that you pushed and pulled her about, punched her in the face and body and finally when she was lying unconscious on the floor you kicked her?"

"Och, it was just the drink, your honour. I don't know nothing about it."

"Well, you'll know all about sixty days in prison."

That was, as far as he could see, the only use prison ever served, to separate and protect society from the criminal.

That was certainly something that had to be done and he was all for long sentences. But as things stood at present these had no remedial effects whatsoever.

By the time cases became "cases" it was, in his opinion, too late. He believed that something could have been usefully done at some point but he suspected the seeds would have to have been planted in early childhood to stand any chance of a good harvest later.

They kept rolling in, mostly long-haired youths of about Joe's age. Not much older. For a moment, thinking of Joe and how near he had come to being in court after his carry-on of the other night, McGouran felt his whole solid fourteen-stone body liquefy with fear.

If only he could make Joe realise how hopeless it was to

step across the line, how it would ruin his life, how he would never be able to get back again and be accepted into decent society. Once the police got to know him they would keep a lookout for him and if anything happened, if anything went wrong in the district, Joe's would be the familiar face.

He would be, literally, a marked man. He would be picked up for one thing after another. The police had a job to do and they did it, with a marvellous and conscientious efficiency.

His hands itched to batter sense into Joe, to force him to make the right choice. But he knew that force was no answer. He only wished it was. The birch, for instance, could be either a brutalising agent or a release from frustrations for the society or the individual who delivered it. But in his experience it had no remedial value to the boy at the receiving end. Indeed it had the exactly opposite effect from the one intended.

Back in his own childhood a boy in the district called Jimmy had received the birch, and the kudos it gave him was something he would never forget. He remembered all the boys in the neighbourhood congregated up a close to examine and admire the scars on Jimmy's back and Jimmy bending over and pulling up his shirt, proudly showing them off.

The boy had been a hero and from the time of his birching onwards was considered and indeed became the toughest youngster in the neighbourhood and the leader of the most feared gang.

Where would Jimmy be now? McGouran wondered. What kind of man had he become?

He could bet his bottom dollar that Jimmy was in one of Her Majesty's prisons right now and had wasted the biggest part of his life in one penal establishment or another.

It was the terrible waste that angered him, and when he thought of Joe, he felt bitter, too.

His mouth turned down and his jaw hardened.

He had done everything humanly possible for Joe. He had given him every chance. Surely to God he would have enough brains to make the right choice? By God, he'd better!

Anger brought an ominous red shadow to his face. His eyes, under their beetling brows, reflected it. He pushed his head aggressively forward to glare at the white-faced youth now standing before him. Then he bellowed, "Well? Guilty or not guilty?"

Chapter Twelve

Joe did not say a word but Wendy heard from the others how they were all going to meet outside the town hall at half-past eleven and wait for the Gunbraes. She did not tackle Joe about it until the afternoon when they went out sketching.

The air was painful with sharp needles of frost and they both wore long scarves and duffle coats with the hoods up. Even so, they were soon bitterly cold sitting on a fallen tree trunk in the bluebell woods with their sketch pads propped up on their knees. Their noses were a bright cherry red.

She gave a big sniff.

"Don't go, Joe. I don't want you to get hurt again."

"Thanks."

"You know what I mean."

"Oh, Wendy, leave it alone. I wish they hadn't said anything. It's none of your business."

Wendy turned her head and peered indignantly round the side of her hood.

"I'm your girl, aren't I?"

"I suppose so."

"Well then!"

"Just because you're my girl doesn't mean I've got to do what you say."

"But it is my business. Please don't go, Joe. You'll get into trouble. Just before your prelims, too."

"Do you think I want to get into trouble?"

"Well, don't go. Please, Joe."

"Aye, all right," he mumbled irritably.

"Is that a promise? Do you mean it?"

"How do you expect me to do a decent composition if you keep nattering away in my ear hole? If you want me to pass my art prelim, shut up!"

After a few minutes' silence, she remarked, "I've got a new dress."

"What's it like?"

"I'll wear it tonight when we go to the pictures."

Another silence followed until she said:

"I wish I wasn't so thin. I eat and eat and never get curvy."

"You're lucky. I wish I was thin."

"But I'm flat-chested. It's terrible."

"One of my big sisters had an exerciser thing. She sent away for it."

"Did it work?"

"I don't know."

"You must know."

"How must I?"

"You've eyes in your head. Did her breasts get bigger?"

"She's married and I don't see her so often now. Anyway she used to wear a padded brassière. She might still, for all I know."

"Do you think it is a good thing, Joe? Do you think it could work?"

He shrugged.

"It said in the booklet it was guaranteed to add up to six inches to bust measurements."

"That's fab! I wish I could have a shot."

"I'll try and get it for you."

"Would you, Joe? Would you?"

"There's a drip on the end of your nose."

She sniffed and tugged up her duffle coat and wriggled about in her efforts to get her hands into her pockets to search for her handkerchief.

Already she could see herself with big, creamy breasts like Raquel Welch. She would wear dresses and sweaters and blouses with low, scooped-out necklines to show her tantalising cleavage.

She could hardly wait to get hold of the exerciser.

"Come on, Joe," she urged after giving her nose a good blow. "I'm frozen and I'm starving for my dinner. Will you bring it tonight?"

"Bring what?"

"The exerciser, stupid."

"If you like. It means going over to her place before my dinner though."

"Well, come on then!"

She felt so happy she forgot all about the fight. Energy scooped her up and carried her off. She grabbed Joe's sketch book from his hands and bounded off with it like a spring-heeled gazelle.

"Be careful with that, you idiot!" Joe bawled and gave chase with long, thumping strides.

Their laughter had an echoing ghost-like quality that curled round trees. And as she flung back her head she could see frosty clouds of breath and brown branches against a pearly sky.

Even hours afterwards, sitting beside Joe in the Rio Cinema with an exerciser in a brown paper bag on her knee, happiness still sent electric currents sparking through her. She could have leapt to her feet and danced and danced.

Life was like that; a high-low swing, a swooping pendulum, a bumping, jumping see-saw. One minute she felt chained in a dungeon of despair from which there seemed no escape, the next minute she had soared away on clouds of joy.

Returning home to Roman Road after the pictures, though, she gradually became aware that she was doing all the chattering. Joe was unusually subdued and quiet.

At the gate of the house she whirled on him in panic, suddenly remembering the fight.

"You're not going to the fight, Joe. You promised."

"I didn't promise."

"You did so."

"I did not."
"You did."
"I didn't."
"Well, promise now, then."
"There's your mother keeking out behind the curtains."
"Come on round the back away from the street lamps and then she won't see us."
"She'll just shout at you to come. I'd better go."
"You're not usually in such a hurry."
"Stop nagging."
"Oh, all right then. Go! See if I care!"
"OK."
"OK!"
He began trudging away but stopped and turned for a moment after only a few paces. He looked anxious and unhappy.
"Cheerio, Wendy."
"Cheerio, Joe."
She watched him disappear up the road toward the Cross before she scuffled her feet slowly and noisily along the gravel of the path. Her hand was on the back door when it occurrred to her that Joe always went the other way down to Hillfoot and from there on to Maryhill Road after seeing her home.
He must be going to the town hall. At first she trembled so much she had to keep clutching at the door to hold herself up. She had wild momentary hopes of calling to her mother and father to run after Joe and help save him. Then bitterness and sadness set in.
Nobody was ever going to help Joe and her.
She flew breathlessly from the house and up Roman Road.
Round the corner on Drymen Road she saw the Bearsden crowd in front of the town hall. There were about a dozen of them including Joe, all bunched together.
A police-car sat in the road nearby and another car and a van were parked across in New Kirk Road.
"Joe!"
She called to him as she hared along and over to his side

of the road without bothering to see if any traffic was coming.

"Beat it!" he growled.

She could see he had gone crimson with embarrassment but she did not care.

"Look at all the police, Joe!"

"Fuck the fuzz!"

Gash Merrilees nudged Joe.

"One of the Gunbraes looked out. He's gone back in to tell the others. I heard there's about fifty of them. That's four to one. Bloody cowards, aren't they? They couldn't have a square go if they tried."

"Here they come!" Joe said. "Run, Wendy. Quick!"

The leader of the Gunbraes was a small man of about twenty but he swaggered out as if he were ten feet tall. His much younger followers came crowding, clanging, jostling close behind him. Then suddenly the bouncers shut the doors and would not let any more out.

Gash chuckled as he and the Bearsden crowd moved forward.

"That's pared the odds down a bit."

Wendy could see that the Gunbraes were startled and taken off guard by this unexpected turn of events and within seconds they were on the ground with the Bearsden boys on top of them.

In the general turmoil Wendy lost sight of Joe but she saw a Gunbrae emerge and stagger towards the police-car that was still sitting at the side of the road. Wildly he tugged at the door-handle in his efforts to get into the car for protection.

But the door was locked and the policemen ignored him.

He was still fighting with the door when Gash Merrilees came up behind him, tapped him on the shoulder and smashed a fist into his face the moment he turned round.

The Gunbrae groaned, thumped back against the car then slithered down it to the ground.

The police waited until the fight was over before moving in.

"Up against the wall!"

All the boys were rounded up, dragged to their feet, and

pushed and prodded towards the town hall. There they were made to stand in a long line with palms flat on the wall and feet as far as possible from it, so that they were balanced in such a way that they could not turn round in protest without losing their balance and falling flat on their faces.

The police searched each one for weapons, then went back along the line asking:

"Where are you from?"

If the answer was "Bearsden", the boy was told to "get away home".

If the answer was "Drumchapel" the boy was ordered into the police van.

Wendy had been told to go home several times as she hovered anxiously near Joe but she ignored the policeman.

Until he said to Joe:

"Where are you from?"

"Maryhill."

"Into the van."

"But it wasn't his fault," she cried out indignantly.

"Get lost," the policeman said.

"I'm not going anywhere without Joe. You can't arrest him just because he doesn't live in Bearsden. It's not fair."

"We're being more than fair to you. Now, be a good girl and go home."

"He's a friend of the Bearsden crowd."

"Do you want your folks to get a fright seeing you taken home in a police-car?"

"How about his folks? How are they supposed to feel when they find him in your police station?"

"That's his worry. He had no right to be here."

"Why not? Is Bearsden holy ground or something?"

The van was packed now and ready to go.

"Less of your cheek. He doesn't belong here. Just you think yourself lucky that you do!"

The love-hate relationship she had with the place burned to a white heat with the whole unfairness of the older generation and especially the injustice their world was dishing out to Joe.

Her eyes protruded in a face gone flour-white.

She would soon see if the fuzz could avoid arresting someone who belonged to the holy Bearsden soil.

"Aw, shut up!" she said, then spat on him.

Chapter Thirteen

Owen . . . Owen . . .

She hated the sound of his name long before she hated him in person.

Owen did this. Owen said that. Owen was so handsome. Owen was so clever. Owen was kind. Owen was generous. Owen was misunderstood. Everyone in the whole camp was jealous of Owen. No one liked or understood Owen. No one, that is, except her husband.

Owen sounded sly. Holy Owen with a crucifix dangling round his neck on a delicate silver chain.

She had hoped that with the end of the war all the wartime nightmares would end. But with real nightmares there was no waking up and the effects of war never ended.

Before returning to Britain Peter had had his hair cut to its pre-war short-back-and-sides. He was thinner. There was an alabaster polish to his skin and his blue eyes cast darker blue shadows that aged him. But apart from that he seemed, at first glance at least, to be the same.

He breezed into the house exactly as he had breezed out of it.

She ran to him with great joy. Her parents were both dead by the time the war finished and she was alone in the villa with its dark, embossed paper and wax fruit and stuffed birds with beady eyes.

"Celia," he had cried out to her, with barely an absent-minded hug of greeting, "meet Owen!"

Owen glanced quickly at Peter then said with a chuckle, "Heard a lot about you, I have!"

"All nice things, I hope?"

Only with a terrible effort of will-power did she succeed in acting out the part of a bright sophisticated hostess. She plied him with drinks and fussed busily in the kitchen preparing a special meal while Peter and Owen talked and laughed together in the sitting-room. Or while Peter showed Owen around.

From all over the house came the strangely twisted speech interrupted by spurts of laughter.

"Very nice, it is . . . Lucky, you are . . ."

She began to feel in the way, an outsider, a stranger in her own house. Indignation flared up. For years she had been dreaming and longing for this homecoming, this first day of reunion with her husband. What right had any man to come and spoil it. She had not been able to address more than a couple of words to Peter in private and they had never kissed. She had practised that first kiss so often and so passionately in her dreams and it was still burning inside her like a thirst that had to be quenched or she would go wild with it.

Alone in their bedroom at last, Peter still did not kiss her.

"How long is he supposed to be staying?"

"That's not a very nice way to speak. The poor chap's just arrived home after being a prisoner-of-war for years."

She felt petty and mean and hated herself but was compelled to go on.

"This isn't his home."

"You know what I mean."

"No, I don't know what you mean, Peter."

How could he put her in such an intolerable situation? She could not quite grasp the reality of it. It was as if they were both acting parts in a play. Now he assumed an aggrieved attitude.

"I'm disappointed in you, Celia. You don't sound the person that I remember at all."

"You do remember me then?"

"You were always so quiet. Don't tell me you're going to turn out to be a nagging wife."

"I only asked a simple question. How long is he going

to stay? I've got to know. There's food to worry about for one thing. It's still rationed, you know."

"You needn't grudge him his food. He has a ration book the same as everybody else and as far as I'm concerned he can stay as long as he likes."

She lowered her voice to a whisper so that Owen could not hear through the bedroom wall.

"I don't like that man. I can't think what you see in him."

"I'm warning you, Celia!" Peter suddenly shouted with an emotion that seemed out of all proportion to the event. He was almost hysterical. "You'd better be decent to Owen. He's my friend. I will not allow you and your small-minded, spiteful, suburban snobbishness to make his life a misery!"

"I'm your wife. How dare you talk to me like that! I've been waiting here for years for you to come home to me and now after all this time we can't be alone and I can't talk to you in private without whispering."

"You're selfish, that's your trouble. You're wailing about being here in a place like Bearsden while that poor man has been going through hell at the hands of the Germans."

"Through hell?" Her whisper stretched into throaty derision. At the same time she could have wept. She did not want to talk like this. She did not mean anything she was saying and she regretted every word as soon as it was uttered.

"Through hell? Don't make me laugh. You and Owen and the rest of your precious theatre group were enjoying yourselves. You loved every minute of it."

"You're mad," he said. "I've heard of jealous neurotic women but this is ridiculous. I wonder what a psychiatrist would say if he heard you talking like that?"

Was she just being selfish and jealous, she wondered. She struggled against her every instinct to view the situation from another, more casual, angle.

Peter had simply brought a friend home with him for a little holiday that was all. It was kind of Peter to want to put Owen up until he found a place of his own. It was only decent and fair to give Owen time.

She squeezed the lid firmly down on her emotions and gave Owen time. She also provided him with a room in her home and scrupulously polite and conscientious attention. Until eventually he said:

"I don't want you running after me like this, girl. There's no need, you know. I learned to cook from my mam. A wonderful cook she was. But plain. Very plain. I learned a few things at the prison camp. I'll cook you a real meal. Peter will help, won't you?"

She tried to smile at the sight of them both working about the kitchen. Edging awkwardly around their smooth purposefulness she kept warning herself that it was wrong to feel jealous. If Owen wanted to cook fancy recipes that he had swopped with Russian and French and Polish and God knows what other nationality of POW—well—fine. Just fine. There could be no denying that the food he produced was marvellous. She had to admire him.

"I don't know how you manage it."

One complicated meal followed another until she was overwhelmed. Her own efforts in the kitchen seemed amateurish and completely inadequate. She found herself apologising for the chicken casserole which had been her speciality, her pride and joy. After sampling Owen's *savarin* she dreaded serving up her homely apple tart. The potato and leek soup that everyone seemed to enjoy before was insipid and unimaginative compared with Owen's lobster *bisque* laced with brandy. Shame and embarrassment had to be swallowed down with each meal and hurt her like a fish-bone stabbing in her throat. Her confidence in her cooking abilities scattered in the winds of panic until she was reduced to kitchen clown. She could not even find anything. Toast burned while she searched in vain for the toast rack. Milk overflowed while she fluttered round in circles trying to think where the custard jar could be.

"I've reorganised the shelves for you, girl," Owen explained. "Makes the cooking easier if everything's organised, like."

Peter said: "He's awfully good, isn't he?"

"I've shifted the washing machine into the scullery. Gives you more room in the kitchen."

"Nothing's too much trouble for Owen," Peter said.

"There's the kitchen knives hanging there in front of your eyes, girl. Didn't want you slicing your fingers off fumbling for dangerous things like that in a drawer."

"There's nothing he wouldn't do for you," Peter said.

The words found no answering warmth in her heart. Only suspicion and ever-growing fear.

To add to her confusion clothes began going missing too. She could not be absolutely sure at first. She was absent-minded and forgetful. Yet often she could have sworn that a certain dress had been hanging in her wardrobe. Or a bra and girdle had been on the bedroom chair. Or stockings in the dressing-table drawer. Each time she would search and search and become more and more anxious and bewildered. Then the next day there the dress would be, hanging in its proper place in the wardrobe. Or the underwear would be draped on the chair exactly as she remembered leaving it. Or the stockings would be tucked neatly in the drawer.

Owen, she decided, must be playing tricks on her. Why he should play such stupid, senseless, ridiculous trick on her, she had no idea. She secretly rehearsed over and over again how she would tackle him about it. Then one evening when the three of them were sitting reading by the fire she suddenly shouted out:

"I've had quite enough of your tricks, Owen. If I've to put up with any more of your sly, sneaky behaviour I'll have to ask you to leave."

He shrugged, turned to Peter and spread out his palms.

Peter got up and came over to stare down at her in bug-eyed silence. She glared back at him with undisguised hatred.

"Oh, of course. You've got to leap to your precious Owen's defence."

"How dare you? How dare you, for no reason at all, speak to Owen like that? He's been nothing but good to you."

"I don't want him to be good to me. I don't want him to be anything to me. Or to you."

"You ought to be ashamed of yourself. That man has practically run this house for you."

"I know. Oh, I know. Don't I bloody know it!"

"Keep your voice down and watch your language. Do you want the neighbours to hear you making a fool of yourself? You ought to be grateful to Owen. He's worked like a slave in this house. Look at the money he's saved us by helping me decorate the place."

"Oh, marvellous. Bloody marvellous," she said bitterly.

"He's never said one wrong word to you."

"Oily bloody Owen."

"You're vicious and spiteful and mad. Quite mad. We were sitting here minding our own business when you suddenly, for no reason at all, burst out with a stream of abuse. I'll never forgive you if you don't apologise to my friend. I'll never forgive you as long as I live."

Owen had lit a cigarette and she could feel his eyes sliding round to her through the drifting smoke. Dark, watchful, amused, sexy eyes.

My God, she thought, he is handsome! The neighbours, her friends, the girls in the salon were always saying: "How lucky can you get, Celia? You've managed to capture two handsome men."

Lucky? Maybe she was going mad.

"Oh, all right," she said. "I'm sorry. I'm sorry."

Owen blew out smoke rings.

"That's all right, girl. No harm done."

"No?"

She stared at him for a long time. Tiny slivers of laughter pricked back at her.

Damn you. She tried to speak with her eyes; to send words straight into his. Damn you. Damn you.

Peter said, "Doesn't that prove how patient and good-natured he is?"

Chapter Fourteen

Peter had talked of his hell as a prisoner-of-war. He could not have suffered any more agony than she did as a prisoner of peace.

She wished to God Owen would go away and give them a chance to lead a normal life.

All her school friends were married and had homes of their own. Sometimes she saw them at the shops, happily harassed with babies and young children and with proud husbands in tow. Sometimes they hailed her and invited her to come to some bridge party or other kind of get-together. They usually included both Peter and Owen in the invitation.

"You mustn't be greedy, darling," they laughed. "It really is too bad of you to try and keep them all to yourself."

But Peter had no interest in going out or in entertaining. He would bring her a box of chocolates and Owen would present her with a bunch of flowers and Peter would say,

"We don't need anyone else, do we? We're perfectly happy as we are."

The only place they ever went to was the church. They were great church-goers, Peter and Owen.

She had to make excuses to friends. Or she avoided them. She went bus runs on her own. She visited the park on her own.

All the time in the house Owen and Peter were together. During the day they both worked in the salon. They had trained together at hairstyling and eventually went into partnership in their own salon where Owen serenaded the customers as he clipped and styled their hair.

"All the customers adore him," Peter told her.

In the evening they gossiped about individual customers they knew but who were strangers to her. Owen mimicked them and she felt ashamed at laughing because of the cruelty he showed. Sometimes Peter and Owen spent long hours in the garage tinkering with or polishing their shared car.

When she attempted to break into their magic circle by

addressing remarks to Peter she had to repeat herself several times before he showed the slightest awareness of her existence. And even when he did turn to her it was at best with a vague irritation. He was completely engrossed in the world he shared with Owen, a world in which she had no part.

Occasionally she would have a coffee morning and chatter brightly with old school friends.

"Aren't you lucky!" they would gasp. "No wonder you always look so well-groomed and never a hair out of place. If your husband hasn't time to give you a fabulous hair-do to keep you perfect, you've that sexy-looking Welshman on tap."

Sometimes she was afraid that if anyone said the word "lucky" to her again she would spit in their face. But instead she managed to laugh and agreed with them. Then she was glad when they went away and she did not need to pretend any more. It saddened her too that she needed help and was unable to communicate her need to anyone. What could she say? If Peter had been spending time with another woman, if his affection and loyalty had been bound up with another woman then everyone would have understood. She would have understood herself.

Was she being over-possessive, neurotic, even a little mad, being jealous of a man?

She was jealous. That much she admitted to herself. Jealousy gnawed at her like a constant pain. She found it increasingly difficult to retain her quiet civilised voice and normally polite manner. More and more often hatred was erupting to coat her words with acid.

"Why haven't you another friend, Owen?"

"Wouldn't it be nice to have a place of your own where you could entertain girlfriends for instance?"

Peter always interrupted indignantly:

"Have you gone crazy or something? Why are you saying stupid things like that. Of course he doesn't want to go. Why should he? He's perfectly happy here."

She wanted to rivet Owen's dark eyes before they

retreated into the creases of his smile. She wanted to say, "This is my home. I want you to go. Get out!"

She did not need to have any reason. She wanted to insist to Peter: "You've got to make a choice. It's either Owen or me."

But she knew he would choose Owen. Every time she dared to say one word about Owen, Peter flew into a rage and insulted her. But it had always been a quiet rage because he did not want the neighbours to hear any more than she did. They had both been indoctrinated since childhood that success was the only yardstick and it had to be seen to exist at every level whether it did or not.

Peter would choose Owen, all right. The certainty was so terrible, so humiliating that it made her feel sick. Who had ever heard of such a ridiculous situation?

Millions of words in articles and correspondence in newspapers and women's magazines gave sympathetic advice on how to deal with "the other woman". If only there were another woman in her case. She might know what to do then. At least she would stand a chance. Never, not once, had she ever read anything to help or advise anyone in her situation. Eventually, in desperation, she wrote to one of the problem pages taking care, of course, to use a pseudonym and to post the letter in town so that there would not even be a Bearsden postmark.

She tried to be scrupulously fair. She detailed in the letter how generous her husband was, how handsome both he and his friend and business partner were and how kind they could both be but . . .

A few days later her letter appeared, rewritten in the same slick facetious style as all the other letters and all the other answers. "Sister, you think you've got *problems*?" was the reply.

She felt foolish and ashamed. People were starving all over the world. People were ill, and dying. She was nothing but a spoiled, middle-class neurotic. She should give herself a shake, snap out of it, think herself lucky.

She looked around her luxurious house and dutifully repeated to herself, "I'm lucky. I'm lucky."

In her mink-trimmed coat and matching mink hat and muffs she strolled along Bearsden's pleasant streets and smiled at friends and marvelled at how lucky she was.

So her husband got on well with his partner. So Owen did interfere in her kitchen. So Peter did not want sex very often. So what? So bloody what? What did she care?

She returned to the house and to her room, and the first thing she noticed when she was hanging her coat back in the wardrobe was that her blue wool dress was gone. She had been wearing it that morning before she had changed into her coffee-coloured silk. She had put it on a padded hanger and slid it in between her red wool suit and her emerald green jersey frock. She remembered. She was not going mad. Trembling with anger she flew along to Owen's room.

The door crashed open and a grotesque distortion of Peter in a dress and stockings and high-heeled shoes flashed, like a horror film too close and larger than life, before her eyes. A pink painted face with a gash of scarlet mouth and arched clown-like eyebrows pricked an instant tattoo in her mind. He was laughing and his laugh continued, but quickened with excitement, when he saw her.

"We were having a bit of fun remembering the old POW theatre group. Peter was marvellous at the drag," Owen said.

"Drag?" she echoed. "Drag?"

She thought Peter looked so pathetic she could have wept for him.

"Come now, girl. You've surely seen pantomime?"

She shook her head. For a terrible few minutes she was afraid that she was going to take root in the room, never be able to move again, think again, speak again.

"Are you all right, girl?" Owen enquired solicitously. "Is there anything wrong?"

He was sitting on the chair beside the dressing-table stripped to the waist. His skin was the colour of candles. Soft fat folds of flesh bulged over the top of his trousers.

Black hairy breasts drooped over black hair curling from a white navel.

Her head ticked to and fro. The open doorway sucked her out of the room. Walls punched her along. Stairs jolted her down. The sitting-room beckoned her, supported her, assured her of the comfort of the whisky bottle and the chair to shrivel into as she drained the glass.

Chapter Fifteen

"Is there something wrong, Mrs King?" shopkeepers asked curiously. "You look as white as a sheet."

"Celia, my dear!" her friends cried out in concern. "You're shivering. Are you ill?"

Ill? If only it were so simple, so easy. What did illness mean except escape to bed, rest, comfort, sympathy and attention.

She was living in a nightmare. Even her tranquillisers and her sleeping tablets no longer had any effect. She kept thinking—"It isn't true. It can't be true. Wendy is not appearing in court at the County Buildings in Bearsden with a crowd of gangsters."

"It's that boy," Peter seethed. "That scruff. That hooligan. That criminal!"

Immediately Wendy leapt to Joe's defence.

"Don't you dare call Joe names. Don't you say anything about him. You don't know him."

"We know enough, m'lady. More than enough. This is the second time he's got you into trouble but it'll be the last. If I see you with that rubbish again, I'll throw you out on your ear. You're not going to ruin my good name and reputation. I've lived in this place all my life and there's never been as much as a whisper against me."

"Oh, I know that!" Wendy cried out, bitterly. "You're too sly to be found out."

Peter's voice dropped to an ominous whisper.

"What do you mean by that?"

Celia felt suddenly light-headed with terror.

"Don't listen to her, Peter. Please. Oh, please. She's caused enough trouble. I can't stand any more."

Wendy lifted her chin. Courage and fear fought a battle for supremacy in her face.

"How about your boyfriend? I could think of a few names for him!"

Her father's hand shot out and smacked across her face.

"I only wish you were half as good, half as kind, as clever, as honest, as upright a character as Owen. You'll never be good enough to lick his boots."

"Oh, charming!" Wendy overflowed with tears. "I've always known that's how you felt. You don't care about anybody except him."

"Wendy!" Celia moaned. "You wicked, wicked girl!"

Wendy began to half sob, half laugh.

"Honestly, Mummy, you're priceless."

"Peter, I feel ill!"

He hurried solicitously over to her.

"Come on, I'll help you upstairs. You'll be all right. Don't let her upset you."

"That's right, Mummy. Just you hide away."

He helped her into the fourposter bed and spread the quilt over her before hurrying back downstairs to make a pot of tea.

Peter was always at his best when she was ill, tucked up in bed at the top of the house in her curtained-off, silent world. He spoke tenderly to her and there was a barely suppressed eagerness about him. He seemed so anxious to please. He brought flowers and sweets and magazines and assured her over and over again that she could stay there as long as she liked.

Often she felt tempted to remain there, shut safely away. It was a blissful escape. It was a pit she must not fall into but kept stumbling towards as the date for Wendy's case came nearer. Each day the thought of Wendy's name appearing in the local paper tormented her.

Then she discovered quite by chance that everyone under

seventeen was classified as a juvenile and names of juveniles were not allowed to be published.

The relief was indescribable. She went down on her knees and thanked God.

The knowledge that her friends and neighbours need never find out gave her the strength to accompany Peter and Wendy to the court. Up until the last moment she had clung to the escape route of bed.

Pity for Wendy's silent, white-faced distress, however, forced her to make a supreme effort.

The child was obviously terrified.

They had made her take a bath that morning and thoroughly brush her hair and tie it tightly back in a ribbon. She wore her short blue coat and navy gloves and shoes and looked quite smart. She walked silently between them, her face like death.

Celia felt as if there were a spotlight blazing down on the three of them, picking them out for all to see as they approached the County Buildings. The path towards the entrance seemed endless and even inside the building Celia was still in a strait-jacket of tension and suspense.

Someone they knew might be here to pay their rates or on other innocent business. What could they do if someone hailed them and stopped to talk? What if, in the middle of a conversation, a policeman called Wendy's name?

As rapidly as possible they hustled her into the waiting-room next to the room that was used as a court. It was bare except for chairs round the walls and very shiny linoleum covering the floor.

Every chair was occupied by either a boy or his parent but an attendant brought more chairs and everyone moved along and made a place.

Silence was broken every now and again by someone talking in a lowered, self-conscious tone because they knew that everyone else had nothing to do but listen.

"There's Joe!" Wendy cried out and made to rise, but immediately her parents' hands shot out and detained her and she crumpled back into her seat.

Celia looked across the room but her attention was caught, not by Joe but by the big-boned figure of his father.

For no apparent reason her heart began to palpitate. Yet the unexpected distress brought with it a strange pleasure. Awareness of McGouran fanned consciousness of herself. She smelled her own fragrance. He was a heavy-shouldered bull and she was a delicate pink-cheeked Dresden figurine.

She moved her legs to display their slender gracefulness. She peeled off her gloves and arranged her small white hands on her lap. Her eyes strayed across the room again.

Again the heart-thumping discomfort.

He was leaning forward, elbows on knees, hands sticking out, one bunched over the other. His eyes clamped on her. She avoided them. Her gaze fluttered down past the biggish nose, the strong square jaw, the muscle-bound neck.

She could imagine his chest and arms a mass of hair. The backs of his hands were hairy.

She imagined his heavy thighs.

Her gaze snapped away and fastened on Joe. He was scrubbed as clean and shining as Wendy and his clothes were of good quality and well-pressed. The brown suit and blue shirt flattered his hair and eyes. But he was big and gross like his father. She could see the animal attraction he must have for Wendy.

It was disgusting.

Her glance flicked to his mother then to the window. His mother looked common. Celia shrank inside with embarrassment at the mere idea of wearing such a mixture of bright colours. And those dreadful candy-floss earrings!

She thought of her own little black coat with satisfaction. Lightly she fingered the pearls at her throat. They had been a Christmas gift from Peter. Every tiny pearl matched the other in size and creamy lustre.

Peter said, "Any minute now!"

Horror rushed back. The air spun with sickly colours. Her skin went cold and pricked with needles. Her strength drained out. It seemed a miracle that she had managed to get here and it would need another miracle to support her in the court and get her safely home.

Once, long ago, she had sat waiting with her parents in the old County Buildings. They had told her she was going to stand trial for being stupid and ridiculous. Everyone would read all about her in the papers, they prophesied the whole of Bearsden would be saying her name and pointing at her and laughing.

They had only been administering their own special brand of punishment. They must have been there on ordinary business that had nothing to do with her. She knew that perfectly well now. Yet the torment had lost none of its agony, and reached its pitch when they went into the courtroom with Wendy.

The certainty that Wendy's misdemeanour could not be reported in the papers did not help.

Cold became heat. Sweat leaked from every pore. Underwear clung wetly. Rivulets trickled from her hair and forced her to keep pressing her handkerchief against her temples.

Wendy, Peter, the McGourans, everyone faded. She was alone, completely obsessed.

Only after they had returned home, only after she assured herself over and over again that it was all over and she was safe, only then did the intensity of her distress begin to fade.

"You'll pay every penny of that fine yourself," Peter told Wendy. "Don't imagine I'm paying out money for you to behave in such a revolting, disgusting . . ."

"Peter, please. It's over now. Let's try and forget all about it. I'm sure Wendy has learned her lesson." Her pleading gaze sought her daughter. "You won't misbehave again, will you, dear? Please darling. I know it's not easy at times. But you will try, won't you? For my sake?"

She could see the pity in Wendy's eyes.

"Yes, Mummy."

"That's a good girl."

Unexpectedly she began to cry.

"Mummy, don't!" Wendy said.

"I'll be all right in a minute, dear. I don't know why I suddenly . . ."

"Well, I do," Peter said. putting a hand on her arm and

leading her towards the door. "You're enough to make anyone weep. I feel like weeping myself after all the worry and humiliation you've made us suffer."

His hand was slender and elegant and beautifully manicured. Looking at it, feeling its softness, she remembered McGouran's hand.

"Celia, you're trembling." Peter's voice caressed her with sympathy. "Come on. Don't you worry. I'll soon have you safely upstairs in bed."

Chapter Sixteen

The bathroom mirror caught Joe by surprise. He stared at his reflection. He had bluish shadows under his eyes. The rest of his face looked pale and drawn.

Funny, he had been all right until after the court. Then he had developed the pains in his head and the frightening double vision.

He thought he was going blind.

He had always worried about whether or not he would have enough talent to be accepted for art school and eventually become a great artist.

Wendy never had the slightest doubt.

"You're ten times better than me, Joe," she always assured him. "You're bound to get a place."

He had always alternated between dreams of greatness and depressing self-doubt, but lack of confidence was one thing, blindness quite another . . .

Coloured shapes flashed before his eyes in time with the pain.

His parents had been nagging on at him as usual.

". . . and the toffee-nosed bitch thinks her precious daughter's too good for you, that's the laugh," his mother said. "Holy Saint Anne, I'll never understand what you saw in that girl, Joe . . ."

"Leave me alone!"

"You've been left too much to go your own way, that's half your trouble," his father accused. "If you went to Mass, and joined some organisation in the church, you'd get on a lot better. It would put some backbone into you. Help you to resist temptation and make you do penance for your sins. It's no use being a weakling in this world. You've got to crush temptation right away."

Joe squinted over at him.

"I don't know what you're talking about."

"You know what he's talking about," his mother said. "That girl's only got to crook her little finger and you're in trouble. You dad's right. We've been telling you for years. You'll never be any use as long as you turn your back on the Church."

"A lot it's helped you to resist temptation," Joe burst out. "While you're in next door supposed to be doing your good deed for Teresa Nolan, you're having it off with her man."

"You dirty liar!" his mother screamed.

He knew she would never forgive him. For years he had watched her kid herself that she was dishing out Christian charity and comfort to Teresa's husband because Teresa was a paraplegic. He marvelled at how self-deceiving people could be.

The pain in his head flared until it blurred his eyes. He saw two of her, two blonde heads, two popping eyes, two mouths twisted with hate.

"You filthy-minded pup. We're not all like you, you know. You and your red-headed Proddy horror with her disgusting habits." A nerve was leaping about her face, and her eyes were shifty as she turned to his father: "He's a dirty liar, Al."

He thought for a terrible minute that his father was going to kill him.

"Get to your room," he said hoarsely. "You've done enough damage for one day."

He was only too glad to escape—first to the bathroom to be violently sick and then to his bedroom where, after closing the curtains, he lay on his bed and tried to draw comfort from the darkness.

He tried to keep his mind off the fear about his eyes. The thing was, if he could not go to art school, he might as well die. There was nothing else he wanted to do. Nothing else he could do.

He thought of the Gunbraes. They never seemed to worry about anything. That was why he and the Bearsden boys envied them as well as hated them.

The Gunbraes were dead gemmy. They never worried about exams. They never cared about being hurt or arrested by the police or about what their parents or anybody thought.

When they came up to Bearsden and paint-sprayed the name Gunbrae over walls or doors, they took their time over it and made a big splash.

It always infuriated the Bearsden crowd to see the Gunbraes' name plastered up on their territory and they felt it was only right that they should make their mark. Yet even the buying of the paint-spray was a furtive agony to the crowd, including himself. The furtiveness intensified to almost unendurable proportions when it came to spraying their slogan. It was supposed to be "Krazy Kross". They felt so compelled to write as rapidly as possible, however, in case parents or neighbours or anybody that they knew saw them, they just scribbled "Krazy X".

In the waiting-room in Bearsden Joe had felt, for the first time, a certain camaraderie with the Gunbraes. He was sharing the same experience. They were on the same side. A common bond had formed between them.

On the way out of the building they had waved and called to him in quite a respectful tone.

"Be seeing you, Beef."

He had given a friendly nod and said, "Aye."

He would rather be friendly with a bloke any day than fight with him.

His father had punched him in the back to hurry him into the car.

"You'll keep clear of that stupid, useless mob, do you

hear? That lot are going to go through Borstal and Barlinnie like a dose of salts. They're going to spend most of their lives thinking themselves smart enough to outwit the law and never managing to be smart about anything. Holy Mother of God, Joe, you've surely more brains!"

He had hated his father for that big fist digging into his back but he had said nothing because he was so anxious to get clear of Bearsden.

The fear of somebody finding out that his father was the law far outweighed the anxiety and strain of appearing in court.

He would never forget being under the same roof with all those Gunbraes, and his father, and Wendy.

Never before in his life had he been so glad to get home. That was why he was surprised to get the headache and the trouble with his eyes.

After a while in bed, the pain subsided and he got up and slunk out of the house. His feet slowed as he passed the Church of the Immaculate Conception. It was a beautiful place of very modern design. The building was shaped like a triangle with the apex serving as a spire.

On the front wall above the long row of glass doors was a huge painting of the Virgin.

He stopped outside the gate and gazed up at the serene figure in the white robe and royal blue cloak with glistening gold radiating from her head and fingers.

"Holy Mary, be a mother to me," he thought. "Don't let me go blind."

He went from there to telephone Wendy and ask her to meet him at Killermont Park.

Often, in his sixteen and a half years, he had felt lonely but all loneliness paled and became a shallow experience compared with the vast black sea of aloneness on which he found himself abandoned now.

He would be at everyone's mercy if he lost his sight.

There was a boy he knew called Sam who lived in Milngavie. He had a heart condition. He was a decent bloke, small and thin and putty-faced, but gemmy. It was a shame how the gangs picked on him. Nearly every week some crowd surrounded him and gave him a going over.

Once, at a dance in the town hall, he had watched a crowd swagger across to where Sam was sitting.

"Do you want to fight us?" the leader had said.

Sam asked. "Fight you, you mean?'

"Naw, us!"

He had joined Sam then and the gang had been a bit taken aback, especially with him being hefty and twice the size of Sam.

"Right," he said to Sam. "Are you willing to have square-go with one of them?"

"Yeah!" Sam agreed.

"Right!" He turned to the gang. "Either have a square-go or fuck off!"

They had shrugged and gone away but afterwards he learned they had got Sam on his road home and nearly battered him to pulp.

It would be a miracle if Sam survived his youth. Joe found it hard enough to claw through the jungle himself and he had health and strength and even height on his side.

Or at least he imagined he had health and strength but now this nightmare about his sight had come to torment him.

A weight of hopelessness and depression made it difficult to breathe. He had to stretch his lungs and wrench up sighs. As soon as he caught sight of Wendy's skinny figure however he hurried anxiously towards her.

She was wearing her duffle-coat and her Bearsden school scarf. Right away he put his arm round her shoulders and she put her arm round his waist and they held tight to each other as they walked into the darkness of the park.

"It's terrible at home," Wendy said. "I told my dad he was a poof!"

"Is he?"

"Yes."

"I told my mother what I thought of her. She'll make my life miserable from now on."

"You're lucky."

"How?"

"You'll be leaving school this summer and going to college. You'll get your grant and you'll be old enough to live in the hall of residence or find digs. I'm only fifteen. I've another year to suffer."

"It's. . . . it's not just them." Miserably Joe kicked at a stone.

"What is it Joe?"

He did not answer and she waited patiently until they reached a sheltered place among some bushes and they both sat down.

Eventually Joe burst out:

"Wendy, I'm awful worried about my eyes."

"Your eyes?"

He told her all that he felt since returning from the court.

"It's all right, Joe." She hugged him in delight. "It's only migraine. My mother sometimes has it. You can get tablets from the doctor to put it away. She never gets it now. The doctor said it was most common in teenagers and highly sensitive, intelligent people. It just means you're sensitive and clever, Joe. I've always known that."

The relief and gratitude he felt was like strong, sweet wine. He felt drunk. He rubbed his nose in Wendy's neck and tickled inside her duffle-coat and they laughed and laughed and rolled over and over.

The world spun around in an intoxication of physical and mental pleasure that became so keen they moaned with the excitement of it. Then it melted into tenderness.

He nursed Wendy in his arms and she sighed, and smiled up at him.

"I love you, Joe."

Chapter Seventeen

It had been revealed at the court that Joe's father was himself a magistrate. Celia could not get McGouran out of her mind. She wondered what it would feel like to be made love to by a big heavy man like that. In her imagination she felt the weight of him. Her fingers traced the thick neck muscles, the big shoulders, the broad chest; a meticulous journey of exploration, building up to a pain of excitement that had to be cauterised from her mind.

She was in anguish about Wendy. She shuddered to think what trouble the child would be getting into next. Peter refused to talk about her any more.

"I've warned her!" He fluttered his hands and averted his head as if the very mention of his daughter's name caused a bad smell and he had to fan it away from him. "I've told her what will happen if she gets into any trouble again. She's out! Out! Finished!"

Yet something had to be done. Wendy was obviously still seeing Joe McGouran and the fact that she was only fifteen and the boy not much older meant the parents of both of them had to accept some responsibility.

If only Joe would stay in Maryhill where he belonged. Surely he could find plenty of friends at his own school and in his own area? Surely that would be so much better and easier for everyone concerned. Perhaps his father could talk some sense into him. His father looked as if he had authority. It was her duty to see that he used that authority. It was ridiculous and no help at all for Peter to keep avoiding the problem or just to threaten to throw Wendy out. The more she thought of Wendy the more vital it became to contact McGouran, and surfing along on a wave of certainty, she phoned up the City Chambers and made an appointment to see him there. But immediately she put down the receiver the wave receded and left her marooned and helpless in the shadow of confused fears.

Why did Wendy have to cause so much trouble and worry? Why couldn't she just be ordinary and normal like everybody else? Only the other day over coffee Mrs

Anderson had been telling her that Elspeth was making a dress. Elspeth had gone with her mother into town and between them they had chosen a pattern and some very pretty pale pink material. Celia could just imagine Elspeth sewing diligently and then emerging, as if straight from the pages of a women's magazine, straight-backed, demure and uncrushable.

It was hard to believe Mrs Anderson's report of earlier rebellious murmurings when Elspeth had wanted to make a long skirt instead of the short dress.

"I just said to her," Mrs Anderson's neck jerked forward, "No, no, Elspeth. There are going to be no long day skirts worn in this house." Her voice became an arrow of accusation aimed straight at Celia. "We've got to be firm, you know, Mrs King. It's for their own good. Is that another new pair of shoes?" she added with a rapid switch of attention. "Aren't you lucky? How lucky you are, my dear!"

A smile of agreement came automatically and stuck to Celia's face but she was thinking about how Wendy had been talking about making herself a long skirt. She had been barely able to supress her harassment.

"Darling, you can't sew."

"I've sewed all the patches on my jeans," Wendy had protested loudly and indignantly. "Anyway, I don't need to sew it. There's great glues now. I can just glue it together."

"Oh, Wendy! Really!"

"What's wrong now?"

"And why can't you keep your hair brushed smooth and tied back from your face like Elspeth's instead of going about like a golliwog?"

Peter came in then, with Owen swaggering behind him.

"That's right. It's absolutely shocking, that hair. One of these days I'm going to march you into the salon, m'lady, whether you like it or not."

"Hello, Owen," Wendy said cheerily. "You might as well move in permanently. You're here often enough, eh?"

Peter flushed with rage.

"Impertinent little madam!" He turned to Celia. "Have you no control over that one at all?"

But before she could say anything Wendy had switched on her transistor and was shuffling jerkily away.

Owen's deep-set eyes creased up and disappeared.

"It's all right, girl. Not to worry!"

Later Peter cornered her in the kitchen and warned:

"I won't have any impoliteness to Owen when he comes here. I want him made to feel welcome, do you hear? He's suffered enough as a child."

"For God's sake! Don't be ridiculous!" she'd burst out in frustration. "Owen's a middle-aged man."

'And you're a middle-aged woman. But you haven't forgotten your childhood. I don't know why you and Wendy don't like Owen. He's always been thoughtful to both of you. He's a good man and a talented one. They certainly think so in the church. He's the best voice in that choir. The minister was just saying he didn't know what they'd do without Owen now. He has such a lovely voice."

"Oh, lovely, lovely. Everything about Owen is just lovely," she had agreed with mouth-twisting bitterness.

For years she had never gone anywhere with Peter without the lovely Owen being there too. Every Sunday he arrived early and the three of them walked together to church. The Bearsden Cross area was always so busy on a Sunday that policemen had to be on special duty directing the traffic. Everyone in Bearsden, it seemed, in cars and on foot flocked to church. Prosperous, well-fed, well-dressed pillars of society smugly aware of their respectability.

Inside dutiful prayers were chanted and gloved hands held up hymn books and faces were raised in praiseful song.

> ". . . Thy bounteous hand with wordly bliss
> hath made my cup run o'er,
> And, in a kind and faithful friend
> hath doubled all my store. . . ."

Afterwards groups stood chatting outside—perhaps about some current nuisance like a strike. Women in pure silk dreses and glossy fur coats complained about the idleness of the working class. And wasn't it a disgrace! Working people were never satisfied nowadays—they were much happier in the old days when they really had to work for what they got and everyone knew their place. Wealthy men shook their heads and sighed and looked wise and said that the working man did not know how lucky he was, and that material things never brought happiness. The women huffed at them impatiently and said housing schemes were full of private cars and colour television sets.

Often Celia and Peter and Owen were part of these groups and Owen would say in that lilting voice that everyone thought so charming: "Don't know what the world's coming to!"

They would go into raptures about his singing in the choir. Like an angel he'd stood and his words streaming up towards heaven.

> "I to the hills will lift mine eyes,
> whence doth come mine aid,
> My safety cometh from the Lord,
> who heaven and earth hath made. . . ."

Celia wished a thousand times over that somehow he would just disappear. But he never disappeared and even the word Owen was enough to bring Peter immediately to life. But try to get him to talk about Wendy and, oh, no, that was a different matter altogether.

She had no choice. She had to keep her appointment with Mr McGouran and depend on him for help and advice.

That morning she bathed and dressed with anxious care, changing her mind several times before deciding what clothes to put on. She had arranged an appointment at the salon before taking a taxi into George Square.

The City Chambers occupied the entire eastern side of the Square and was an impressive building. The style was a free and dignified treatment of Italian Renaissance. Over the main entrance the sculptured frieze had the City Arms and symbolic figures depicting Religion, Virtue and Knowledge, embodying the idea of the older form of the motto: "Let Glasgow Flourish by the Preaching of the Word."

Celia entered through the revolving glass doors and found herself in a beautiful pillared loggia of granite, stone, marble and mosaic. Rich shades of pink, blue, grey, black and red blended harmoniously and gleamed as if every pillar and every inch of floor, walls and ceiling had been polished.

A uniformed council officer strolled towards her.

"Can I help you?"

"I have an appointment with Bailie McGouran."

"Oh, yes, he left word. He's expecting you. Would you take a seat over there and I'll let him know you're here."

She arranged herself gracefully on the chair and then after the council officer went away she eased open her handbag to steal a surreptitious glance at herself in the mirror of her powder compact. With an effort she resisted the urge to touch up her lipstick or powder her face. Instead she just checked that she had a clean handkerchief before quietly closing her bag and fixing her attention on one of the pillars. She concentrated prayerfully on it. Somehow she had never quite mastered the art of yoga meditation but she kept trying.

The echo of McGouran's heavy feet approaching across the marble floor loudened and strengthened the beat of her heart. She could not bring herself to look at him until his broad frame blocked her view of the pillar.

He stuck out a big paw.

"Sorry to keep you waiting, Mrs King."

"I know you're very busy." She rose, her hand still in his. "I feel guilty taking up your time like this. I hope I haven't made you interrupt a meeting or something."

He glanced at his watch.

"As a matter of fact I was thinking of going for an early lunch. Would you like to join me?"

"Oh, well . . . I . . ."

He gripped her elbow and steered her towards the door.

"I know a place where we can get a decent steak."

"I wanted to talk to you."

"Plenty of time over lunch."

Before she could reorganise her thoughts she was hustled outside and along the busy street. She was aware of a keen pleasure, of an acute physical thrill at each point of contact with McGouran. Where his hand cupped her arm the two pieces of flesh seemed to be communicating with each other loudly, clearly and urgently; there was the same immediacy, the same urgency when her hip or leg brushed against his.

The street, the other pedestrians, the noisy traffic were only an artificial backcloth to the reality of McGouran and herself. The restaurant was the back room of a pub with concealed lighting, highland murals and a dark green tartan carpet. She savoured the warmth and intimacy of it and the thick smells of whisky and beer and steak and onions.

McGouran ordered a sherry for her and whisky for himself. Then he fixed her with a stare from under shaggy brows.

"Well?"

Everything about him seemed to her the essence of masculinity. His Roman nose, his aggressive bull neck, the big paw gripping the whisky tumbler, the heavy thighs stretched wide under the table, so close that if they clamped shut they could imprison her own.

She stared back at him with a panic of need beginning to crack and crumple her stiff mask.

"You wanted to talk to me," McGouran said.

"I don't know what to do."

"What about?"

She peered down at the glass in her hand. Amber-coloured liquid slopping violently this way and that, in danger of spilling over. She secured the glass on the table.

"Wendy. I'm so worried. She's only fifteen."

"Joe's only sixteen."

"I know. I know. They're both too young. They've their whole lives before them. They shouldn't be so serious just now."

"I want Joe to be serious. He's been fooling around long enough. It's time he grew up and concentrated on his career."

"I mean about each other."

"Are they so serious?"

"I think Wendy is, and I don't want her to get hurt."

"Joe has his faults but he's fundamentally a good boy. And," he levelled a finger at her, "I don't want him to get hurt either."

"I thought perhaps if you could talk to him."

"Warn him off?"

"He'd listen to you."

McGouran leaned back with a humourless laugh.

"Mrs King, you just concentrate your attention on your own. The girl's your responsibility. You watch her. You keep her in line. Leave me to worry about Joe."

Chapter Eighteen

"Thank you for the lunch."

Her voice was soft and she had a startled look which he found appealing.

He stuck out his spade of a hand. Hers felt like the petal of a flower. He was suddenly reluctant to let her go.

"Look," he said. "How about coming back into the Chambers for a few minutes? Have a look around."

He watched her hesitate. She was no longer young but she was still an attractive woman. Her grooming was immaculate. From the top of her glistening black hair to the toes of her shoes she was perfection. Even her perfume seemed exactly right with its delicate, unobtrusive fragrance.

Her eyes had become guarded, though, and there was a stiffness about her.

"I've never actually been in the City Chambers before today."

"That's a terrible confession for a Glaswegian to make. Come on, I'll show you around and write you out a ticket to get into a meeting of the council."

"Well . . . I . . . I . . ."

She fixed a blank gaze on some point over his left shoulder.

"Come on!" Firmly he cupped her elbow in his hand and propelled her across the road. "It'll be a new experience for you."

The touch of her excited him and he kept a grip of her arm, every now and again increasing the pressure of his fingers into her flesh.

Pride stretched his chest and gave him a peacock swagger as he noticed his colleagues' surreptitious glances of envy as he walked with her inside the Chambers. His pride encompassed the place too.

"Italian marble!" He indicated the grand staircase.

"It's beautiful." She admired everything he showed her but every now and again her gaze strayed to him. No so much to his face but to his body and his hands. "She's lusting after me," he kept thinking.

"I never realised . . ." Her gaze wandered up to one of the ornate ceilings.

"A bit different from the first council hall."

"Where was that?"

"At the corner of the High Street and Trongate. The ancient Tolbooth there had to serve as a prison and a council hall. That's not the same one that's there today. It's the third, but they were always on the same site and built to much the same design. Originally they had the stocks outside. The gallows were nearby."

"The gallows?" She gave a delicate little shudder.

He thought, "I could make you shudder all right!"

"Oh, yes. It was a permanent erection in the Loan leading to the Ramshorn. I'll show you some other time if you like. They used to have branks beside the stocks for nagging women."

"Branks?"

"A kind of iron mask with a metal gag."

She grimaced but kept studying intently walls and ceilings and paintings and carvings and him as they moved along corridors and in and out of rooms.

The woman was definitely over-sexed. He wondered if the daughter was the same. Joe had better watch himself right enough.

"Eventually the Tolbooth wasn't big enough and they built a grand new place in the Saltmarket at Glasgow Green," he told her. "The cells there were so encased with iron that for the first time in Britain criminals didn't need to be in chains. The council left that place to jail and court house business and moved to another new building in Wilson Street. But Glasgow kept growing so fast and so many new departments were needed they had to move again. And the walls weren't dry in that place when they bought the land that we're standing on now."

"We're rather a mixture, aren't we? We've absorbed so many different types over the years. People from the Highlands and Ireland and Italy and India and Pakistan . . ."

"Well, you know what they say . . ."

"What?"

"The only pedigrees in Glasgow are in the Dog Show!"

She laughed and it was a joy to see the way she tipped her head and melted her eyes in gratitude as if he had done her a favour by saying something funny.

It made him feel good. He shoved an impulsive arm round her shoulder as he jerked open the door to the banqueting hall and pushed her inside.

The beat of her heart pounded at every point of contact. She took a cigarette from a silver case, lit up, smoked in quick little bursts and moved away from him.

"The ceilings, the chandeliers, everything is quite fantastic. Thank you for showing me all this."

A bell began ringing loudly and continuously throughout the building.

"That's the meeting. Come along the councillors' corridor and I'll write you a ticket and have someone take you up in the lift to the public gallery."

She became breathless and flushed trying to keep up with his long purposeful strides. "Why 'councillors' corridor'?"

"Well, we stand around talking here. It's handy for the meeting hall and this is where our mail is kept."

He indicated rows of pigeon-holes before getting a card from the table, putting her name on it and signing it.

She took it in a gloved hand, examined it then thanked him.

"The council officer will take you up in the lift and show you where the gallery is."

He nearly said he would see her after the meeting but managed to hold back the words.

Maybe he would, and maybe he would not.

He was still thinking about her when the council officer in a scarlet tail-coat and white bow tie came strutting in carrying the golden mace and calling out, "Ladies and gentlemen, the Lord Provost!"

Everyone stood up as the Lord Provost in his gold chain of office followed the officer in; behind him came the City Treasurer and Town Clerk.

A raised platform held the carved, throne-like Provost's chair and in front of it, forming a large semi-circle, were the rich wood and red leather-upholstered seats of the assembly. On the ledge in front of every seat blossomed a pink carnation, a gift to each member of the chamber from the Parks department.

The Provost arranged himself in his chair, the council officer placed the mace on a table in front of him, and everyone settled down.

As the Town Clerk began to read the minutes, McGouran glanced up at the public gallery. Celia's eyes were glued to him as if he were a witch doctor who had cast a spell on her.

Automatically he flicked over the pages of his agenda. Pages rustled and agitated like a swarm of birds all over the large hall while the voice of the Town Clerk rattled on like an auctioneer in a sale-room.

"Number double two, three, eight . . . the minutes of the housing committee . . .

"Number double two, seven, five, paragraph five, marked 'C' . . .

"Number double two, nine, six . . . the minutes of the police committee . . ."

McGouran found it difficult to concentrate. He leaned forward, his mouth set hard, his neck thrusting aggressively, his brow creased. The consciousness of Celia's eyes boring into him disturbed him, but irritation at the long-winded vagueness of a councillor eventually tossed her out of his mind. He erupted with a roar: "Will somebody please tell Councillor Andrews what he's moving!"

He got up, fingers hooked in waistcoat, and waiting a moment for the laughter to die down. Then his rich Glasgow voice lifting up with sarcastic questioning, addressed his opponent who happened to be a lawyer.

"Lord Provost, is my beloved legal adviser from the opposite side of the house aware . . ."

His bushy brows came together in mock sternness at the ensuing laughter. He enjoyed the cut and thrust of debate and the ability he had to electrify the proceedings. He could make them angry, or make them laugh. He never failed, one way or the other, to command attention. In the middle of his speech he swung round to deal with the councillor who was bobbing up and down and trying to interrupt.

"Be quiet and enjoy this." He fixed a beady eye on his lawyer opponent. "You're getting it for nothing . . ."

"A point of order," the councillor insisted, bobbing up again.

"Sit down, man!" McGouran roared.

The councillor immediately sat down but he turned towards the Provost.

"Provost, I appeal for your protection."

At once everybody in the hall stamped their feet and cried out in a broad Glasgow accent, "Send fur the polis!"

McGouran wondered how the elegant, gently-spoken Mrs King was surviving the proceedings. He decided against finding out.

Later he went home and read his evening paper and ate his dinner and tried to blot the woman from his mind, but already in his imagination he had stripped the clothes off her and they had coupled violently.

As soon as he could, he went to church and confessed to bad thoughts.

He knelt and with lowered head and clumsily clasped

hands recited six Our Fathers and six Hail Marys. He finished with an earnest *Confiteor*.

"I confess to Almighty God, to Blessed Mary, ever a Virgin, to Blessed Michael the Archangel, to blessed John the Baptist, to the holy Apostles, Peter and Paul, and to all the Saints, that I have sinned exceedingly in thought . . . through my fault, through my fault, through my most grievous fault. Therefore I beseech the Blessed Mary, ever a Virgin, blessed Michael the Archangel, blessed John the Baptist, the Holy Apostles, Peter and Paul, and all the Saints to pray to the Lord our God for me."

Joe was in when he got back and Biddy was nagging at him.

"You lazy big good-for-nothing slob, what do you think this is, a hotel run just for your benefit? It's high time you did something to earn your keep."

"I'm supposed to be studying for my Highers." He turned to McGouran. "Dad, how am I supposed to pass my Highers if I don't get the peace to study?"

"Study, my arse!" Biddy sneered. "He's been out all night with that Proddy girl."

McGouran glanced at her with distaste.

"Must you always be so coarse? Especially in front of the boy." He swung on Joe, "And you just watch it! You were warned to keep away from her."

"Coarse now, am I?" Biddy gasped. "Who do you think you are? What gives you the right to come in here and look down your big ugly nose at me?"

Her blonde hair had been enthusiastically back-combed and stuck straight up, as if electrified. Orange-tinged make-up accentuated her enlarged pores and stopped at her jaw. He could see the coloured line.

Once, long ago, before she had developed a weakness for cream cakes, she had been quite a pretty woman.

"You're the one who's ugly!" he said bitterly.

"Say that again," Biddy challenged. "Say that again!"

Joe got up with a sigh and made for the door.

"What do you think you're sighing for?" McGouran

called after him. "You just watch it, lad. I'm warning you. If you don't watch it, there's trouble ahead!"

Chapter Nineteen

A whole new world opened up before Wendy.

It felt like taking drugs, only with none of the side effects.

Drugs held no particular interest for her and Joe never touched them, although they both knew any drug could be purchased within the hour in a public house in Glasgow.

Some of the boys and girls had experimented with Purple Hearts and cannabis. Others dissolved aspirin tablets in bottles of Coke and one boy she knew heated cleaning fluid and sniffed it like an inhalant. He said it made him feel drunk. He went wild, he said, and had a great time.

In odd depressed and despairing moments Wendy had been tempted to give it a try. But her depression always changed quickly to elation and there was never any real need.

Especially after she started going with Joe.

She felt certain that no drug on earth could induce the swoony euphoria she was floating in now.

Her perceptions heightened. Never before had she realised what a beautiful place Bearsden was. Trees and bushes rustled over garden walls. Yellow banks of daffodils delighted the eye. From every other lamp-post flowers overflowed from hanging baskets.

There were four lovely old churches within a stone's throw of Bearsden Cross.

Not so long ago when someone tried to open a pub and was refused a licence by the Bearsden magistrates, the decision was defended in the papers with the words, "Bearsden is a sleepy hollow where the residents only go to church or bed . . ."

It was really a marvellous place. Ten minutes in one direction took you to lush green countryside and quiet wooded retreats. Ten minutes in the other direction and you were in the City of Glasgow.

Glasgow was marvellous.

The countryside was marvellous.

Every morning she awoke and stretched herself, legs wide, heels digging, arms straining high.

She felt ravenous. Birds cheeped excitedly. She danced and sang her way downstairs.

She loved Joe.

She loved everybody.

"Good morning, Mummy!" Hugs and kisses and happy laughter. "Good morning, Daddy!"

Minutes passing, tantalisingly slow. Only existing in waiting space, until it was time to meet Joe.

They chattered feverishly to each other. They had so many plans for the future.

"Wait, wait, please, Wendy, it's my turn now!" Joe shouted at the top of his voice in his effort to get her to stop talking and allow him to have his say. "I've drawn this plan of a house. If I plan it, you see, that'll save us paying an architect. See, it's pretty good. But of course, once I've had a bit of training at art school I'll be able to do a better one."

In an ecstasy of admiration, she clasped her hands.

"Joe! Oh Joe!"

"You like it?"

"Oh, yes!"

"See, the big windows? And the kitchen? Everything'll be fitted and streamlined of course. And we'll have cream walls all through the house and thick fawn carpets."

"A coloured bathroom suite, though."

"OK."

"And one of those long, luxuriously padded settees. And I'll wear a glamorous gold lamé trouser suit. Gold would tone down the red in my hair wouldn't it."

"Your hair's great. Just great."

She sighed. "Oh Joe!"

"Of course, it'll have to wait a year or two. You're only fifteen."

"Fifteen and a half."

"And I'm sixteen and a half."

"Nearly seventeen."

"Yes. But I've art school to get through."

"You'll do it, Joe."

He eyed her cautiously, hopefully.

"Do you think so?"

"Of course! And you'll have your grant, don't forget."

"Oh, yes!" He brightened. "That's great, isn't it? I'll be independent then, Wendy. I'll be able to take you places and buy you things."

She flung her arms round his neck, her mouth eager to find his.

"I think your breasts are getting bigger," Joe said, cupping one in his hand.

"Do you think so?" Delighted, she hitched up her jersey to have a look. "Do you really think so, Joe?"

"Well, it never did that before." He wobbled it. "It was just a wee fried egg."

She squealed and giggled and wriggled and he tickled her and she tickled him until they both had tears in their eyes and were breathless.

Then he hugged her until she nearly cried out in pain.

"Oh, Wendy, I love you," he said.

They made all sorts of detailed plans of the house and settled on a complete colour scheme for each room.

Going into town became fun. Every Saturday they spent hours window shopping. They pressed their faces to the glass and pointed and argued about what particular articles would be best for their needs.

They went for a coffee or a Coke and sat for ages, hunched over the table making laborious lists of requirements of the layout of furniture in different rooms.

Joe talked about how one day he would paint portraits and people would get to know his name and pay fabulous prices to have their picture painted.

They would both do paintings for the house of course, and a few pieces of sculpture.

She was rather good at heads.

"I'll do you head, Joe. I'll start practising now. I'll do lots of sketches, then lots of heads until I make a really fab one."

Joe stared at her very seriously.

"I'll never be able to do justice to you. I'd like to paint you and I will try. But . . ."

"You're going to do great, Joe."

He held her hands; fondled them, examined them minutely.

"I'd be no use without you."

"You'll never be without me."

His fingers gently traced the shape of her nails.

"Promise?"

"Of course, dopey!"

He looked up, uncomfortable with embarrassment but trying to swagger it off.

"Good job you said that. I was ready to land one on you if you hadn't." He bunched his fist and gently stabbed it against her nose. "There's only going to be one boss in our house."

"Yes, Joe."

She giggled then sighed.

"It's great to be happy, isn't it?"

He nodded.

"Can you imagine us, Joe—painting in our own studio, in our own house?"

It was his turn to sigh.

"Yeah!"

After a few minutes' silence he said, "We'll have flowering cherry trees in the garden, eh?"

"And rhododendron bushes."

"Yes, but they'd have to be at the end of the garden, not too near the house because they attract midges."

"Do they?"

His store of knowledge and his cleverness never ceased to amaze her. Sometimes she felt there was nothing Joe did not know or could not do.

But even if Joe had not been the best-looking, cleverest,

kindest, most talented, most fab boy in Glasgow, she would still have loved him.

She was so happy she hardly noticed that her period had not come for a couple of months.

Then she felt a bit sick and she thought she had better mention it to Joe.

His face went white. He looked a bit sick himself.

"Do you think you're going to have a baby?" he asked, half fearfully, half incredulously.

"I don't know," she smiled. "And I don't care—as long as it's like you."

His face gradually relaxed. His eyes softened and brightened.

"Hey, I quite like babies. I've never told anybody else but . . . I think they're no' bad."

Wendy sighed.

"I think they're fab."

"We won't get the usual pink or blue things for it, will we?"

She made a face.

"Some people have no imagination."

"How about orange? That would be a nice contrast to the fawn carpets when it's crawling around."

"I can just see it!" She clapped her hands in delight. "Joe, you're marvellous! Everything's marvellous!"

Tenderly he buttoned up her duffle coat and wrapped her school scarf around her neck.

Then they slowly, dazedly, walked home.

Chapter Twenty

Celia had to get Owen out of the house. It had become an obsession with her.

Owen was a bad influence on Peter. Peter would be perfectly all right if it were not for him. They would be a normal, happily married couple just like any other if only Owen were not there.

Her miscarriage had come as a peculiar blessing in disguise. She had been suddenly whipped off to hospital and lying there alone in that strange white bed, a way of getting rid of Owen had come to her.

Peter arrived in visiting hour and the nurse showed him into the little private room with beaming approval. He was carrying a bouquet of flowers and a large tray of fruit artistically wrapped in ruby-coloured cellophane.

He said, "We'll soon have you home again."

"I wonder."

"What do you mean?"

"I was thinking of speaking to the doctor. It's time I spoke to someone."

There was a tiny pause. Then Peter smiled and murmured smoothly:

"About what?"

"I've had too much to upset and worry me. That's why I'm lying here like this."

"I know you've had too much to do," he soothed. "And I'm sorry. I should have realised before. I'll get you a home help. Someone to come in for a few hours every day. It would be company for you, too. That'll make all the difference. You've no need to worry."

"I don't need a home help. But I do need people to talk to. I feel I want to talk and talk. I'm going to start with the doctor. I wonder if he will agree that I've nothing to worry about once he knows all the circumstances? I nearly died, you know, Peter. How is Owen, by the way?"

Peter's eyes became shifty.

"Oh, he's fine. It was he who sent you the flowers." Tentatively he held them up. "Aren't they gorgeous?"

She ignored them. Her stare never wavered from his face. Her eyes branded him with unspoken words. Gossip! Scandal! Ruin! Jail!

After a long pause he managed reluctantly, miserably:

"He's leaving. Didn't I tell you? Leaving the house.

Going to live somewhere else. He's found a place of his own."

"I'm so glad for him, darling," she said weakly. "It will be so much better for him."

She felt like sinking through the bed with relief.

She would never have been able to carry out her veiled threats. The mere idea of their private problems being made public appalled her. It did not bear thinking about.

Anyway she loved Peter and did not want to harm him or cause him any unhappiness. She felt protective towards him. She saw Owen as a sort of Svengali who had put the evil eye on her husband. She believed Owen had taken advantage of Peter's good nature. He had taken up too much of Peter's time and attention. That might have been all right if Peter had been single, but a married man had obligations to his wife. Loyalties had become confused, that was all.

She returned home leaning on Peter's arm. He opened the front door with his key and guided her gently in. She could not believe that the house was empty. They were actually, at long last, alone.

Tears of gratitude came to her eyes. She sobbed weakly. "I'm so glad to be home. I'm so glad."

Peter plucked his handkerchief from his pocket and wiped her eyes. "You're ruining your make-up. Sit down and relax. I'll go through to the kitchen and make you a nice cup of tea."

She could not stop weeping but he gave her a couple of aspirins with the tea and that helped calm her down. How kind and gentle he was, she thought.

He insisted that she ought to go upstairs to bed for a rest. She laughed feebly.

"I've had enough of resting in bed in the hospital."

But she did as he told her because it was such a joy to feel that at last she was the object of his concern, his sympathy and his attention.

Her joy was short-lived. As they entered the bedroom she saw that his belongings had disappeared.

"Where are you sleeping?"

"Don't worry about me. I'm all right in Owen's old room. I thought you'd sleep better and be happier on your own."

He led her by the arm over to the bed as if he were going to introduce her to somebody.

She moved in a daze. The miscarriage had left her weak and shaken. It was too soon for her to be able to deal with any more problems.

She leaned her head against him.

"I love you."

"Come on now." He became breezy and efficient. "Into bed with you. Slip that dress off while I unpack your nighty."

With trembling hands she slipped off all her clothes then stood feeling strangely ineffectual and helpless in her nakedness. She stared at herself in the mirror. Her body was slim, her skin milky and unwrinkled. Yet she seemed to have aged. A forward slope to her shoulders was almost a cringe. Her body had acquired the feeble look of an old woman.

Peter brought her nightdress and whisked it over her head. Then he flung back the bedclothes.

"In you go!" he sang, then busily tucked the covers around her. "Now just you lie there and don't worry about a thing."

She lay motionless after he went away and left her alone in the room. Now her reflection was propped up by a heap of pillows. She saw huge dark eyes under a blob of black hair. They stared fixedly like a sad painting.

It had taken her a long time to recover. Peter, it seemed, would have been perfectly happy to keep her in bed forever.

"You're not strong. You need looking after."

More to please him than anything else she had allowed day after day to flow past while she lay like a piece of flotsam that had been trapped in a forgotten corner.

Eventually she could not bear the isolation any longer.

Before Peter had time to bring up her breakfast, she went downstairs. He was sitting in the kitchen happily reading the paper and munching toast. In the brief moment when she looked at him before he turned round, it struck her how endearingly familiar he was. All her life she had known him. She had known those long lean hands with their fine fuzz of golden hair when they were pink and chubby. She remembered that body when it was small and wiry inside a blue blazer and short grey flannel trousers. His shoelaces had the habit of working loose and he was always tying them and tugging up his socks. He had been a bright active busy little boy, always talking, always doing something. She remembered his shock of golden hair and his eager eyes and the way he used to suck his teeth and pick them with his tongue.

He was as familiar as a brother. Yet when, surprised, he whirled round, she saw the eyes of a stranger. It was a terrible experience, an experience of only a brief second, a brief second that was to haunt her many times to come.

"Celia!" He jumped to his feet and hurried towards her. "Have I been taking too long with your breakfast? I'm sorry. I didn't realise you were awake."

She smiled at him.

"I'm reporting back on duty. I've been shockingly lazy for far too long."

"Nonsense! On you go, back upstairs."

"No, I'm all right now."

She prayed they would both be all right.

He was wiping his mouth with his napkin, his eyes not meeting hers.

She said painfully:

"Peter, we are going to try again, aren't we? I want to have your baby. Next time it will be different."

"Yes, of course." He flung his napkin down and glanced hurriedly at his watch. "My God, look at the time and I've a hundred and one perms today. I'll have to fly."

Somehow they had to keep trying to build a good relationship, a good marriage. Surely there was no valid reason why they should not succeed.

In desperation she whipped her mind into a flurry of action. She would replan and redecorate and refurnish the bedroom. She would make it the most attractive, the most inviting of places.

Her spirits began to soar with hope again.

She would buy a new bed. A double bed, a four-poster bed and she would drape it and perfume it. She would buy new feminine frilly nighties. She would attract Peter, tempt him, excite him until he just could not bear to be without her.

Chapter Twenty-one

"Why don't you want me to be with you?" Celia wondered how long she could continue speaking in such a light, casual tone. She took another librium capsule. They were supposed to help but she noticed she was taking them more and more often.

"Celia," Peter soothed. "You'd hate it."

"Hate a holiday in Paris?"

"It's a business trip."

"With Owen?"

"He's business. Celia, what's come over you? You don't seem yourself at all. I've been on these International Hairdressing dos lots of times and you've never made such a fuss before."

"I'm not making a fuss."

"Anyway, there's Wendy. You can't take her away from her schoolwork just now, can you? Right in the middle of her exams?"

Gently she nursed her hands. She smiled.

"I suppose not."

He went away whistling. She could hear him chatting to Owen in the kitchen then his footsteps tripped gaily upstairs with Owen's measured tread creaking the floorboards after him. Their laughter excited the atmosphere.

Soon they were back in the sitting-room clutching cases, glancing at wrist watches, eager to be away to catch their plane. Peter blue-eyed and lean-faced, his hair thinning and fading. Owen, still with his jerky swagger and with the same thick black curls.

Peter said, "Now, are you sure you'll be all right? Have you got everything you want?"

She felt like exploding into hysterical laughter. Peter was really very funny. Sometimes he seemed like a child, a little boy who did not mean any harm but who had never grown up.

"I've always survived before." Bitter sarcasm escaped with a pencil of cigarette smoke. "I suppose I'll survive again."

He looked offended.

"There's no need to use that tone of voice."

With a restless impatient movement, Owen lit a cigarette. His eyes began straying towards the door.

"Owen's getting impatient," she said.

As usual Peter leapt to his friend's defence.

"You've no call to start picking on Owen. He's never said a wrong word to you."

"That's right. You haven't, have you, Owen?"

Owen grinned and slid her one of his sideways looks. "Very fond of you, I am."

"You'll miss your plane," she said.

Peter hesitated, in need of reassurance, desperate for the normal status quo to be re-established before he left. Almost as desperate as she was.

"You're all right, then?"

She puffed at her cigarette and smiled and said gently, "Of course. Have a nice time."

As usual she went to the window and waved them off. Then she poured herself a stiff whisky. She kept tipping the glass and sipping at it like a baby with a bottle until it was finished. Then she helped herself to another.

At one time, not long ago, she had become worried about her drinking habits. Of course, she was not an alcoholic or anything dreadful like that, but it was surprising how easy the habit of drinking for comfort could be acquired and how often one needed comforting.

Sometimes she yielded to the temptation several times during the day when she was alone. It was at night, however, that it began to be a problem. She could not sleep. Sleeping tablets were a waste of time. In restless desperation she would slip downstairs for a night-cap and then take another to make sure, and then decide to take the bottle back to bed—just in case!

One night she had been so intoxicated she had stumbled into Peter's room and collapsed, moaning, on top of him.

Later she felt so dreadfully ashamed she had never been nearer committing suicide. She made light of the incident, of course. Raging toothache had driven her to gulp down some whisky, she explained, and after drinking it she felt dizzy and remembered no more.

He had told Owen about the incident and she would never forget Owen's eyes glimmering with laughter.

"You want to watch the whisky, girl. Dangerous stuff, it is!"

Two or three different occasions had indicated to her that Peter confided everything to Owen. She wondered how often they laughed together about something she had said or done.

She could not bear to think about it.

Her whisky escape route was too shameful and dangerous, however. It only needed an unexpected caller during the day or some emergency during the night and people would find out.

That was why she had taken up yoga. But now the winter session was over and the class would not be meeting again until autumn. Practice was the thing, of course. She did try practising on her own but somehow without the cheerful guidance of the instructor and the company of the other ladies in the class it was not the same.

In the autumn everything would be all right. So many different classes and social activities started then. It was now she dreaded. Right now, when Peter and Owen were away enjoying themselves and Wendy was out enjoying herself and the house was quiet.

After refilling her glass she wandered around, nursing it

and rolling it between her palms. Every now and again she raised it and took a sip.

The house shone darkly with many layers of varnish and polish. The curtains, the furniture, everything looked unused. Not a thing was out of place. Each room looked like a photograph from *Good Housekeeping*. Every item, every place of every item, could be checked in some quality magazine and its correctness and good taste defended on that basis.

There were no paintings or books or anything visible to indicate the character or personal taste of the occupants.

She lit another cigarette, then switched on the radio. Cigarette poised in one hand, whisky glass in the other, she began to sway in time to the music. It was as if it were caressing her. She closed her eyes. The whisky was blotting everything out. Staggering a little she went over to the cocktail cabinet and filled up her glass again.

She might as well do the job properly.

Complete oblivion. Nothing less.

In a minute or two she would take the radio and the bottle up to bed. She would lock her bedroom door so that even if Wendy decided to look in to say good night she would not be able to see her. Not that Wendy ever did look in to say good night. Wendy went out early and came in late and never said where she was going.

The thought had barely muzzed through her mind when Wendy took shape before her eyes. She was an awkward child. Lovable yet nerve-rackingly unpredictable. And so untidy.

Celia giggled and swayed and clutched at the back of a chair for support.

"What a ghastly sight!" Wendy's hair was too awful for words. Bright red and thick and long with frizzy waves all over. Her face was a little white button with large emerald green eyes staring over a high nest of school scarf and a shapeless duffle coat.

"Mummy!"

"You sound shocked." Celia giggled again. "That's funny, don't you think?"

"I've brought Joe home to meet you and Daddy."

"Daddy's flown away." She fluttered her hand and dropped her cigarette on the carpet. "He's away to open the golden gates with Saint Owen."

A male form bent down in front of her, picked up her cigarette and held it out to her.

For a hazy, heart-thumping second, she thought it was McGouran.

She touched the broad shoulders and made her fingers walk up the strong neck.

"Mm . . . you're quite something. Do you know that?"

"Mummy!" Wendy wailed, near to tears. "You're drunk and horrible. Leave Joe alone."

"Can you dance, Joe?" She took a sip of her whisky and ogled him over the top of the glass. "Can you?"

He looked sheepish.

"Yes."

"Well, come on then!"

She began to sway and shake her head. Wendy hurried over and gripped Joe's arm.

"I brought Joe to meet you and Daddy."

"Daddy's away-up-a-ky."

"We had something important to tell you and now you've spoiled everything. You always spoil everything for me."

"I always . . . *I* always . . . spoil everything . . . for *you*?"

Celia laughed so much she nearly fell over. Joe caught her just in time.

She sighed and rested her head against his chest.

"Big McGouran! The big rough tough Glasgow bailie!"

Wendy began to cry.

"What's she talking about now?"

"I don't know," Joe answered miserably. "Can't you get her to bed or something?"

"You get me to bed," Celia murmured. "You get me to bed."

"You're horrible," Wendy sobbed. "I hate you."

Joe tried to encircle Wendy with his free arm.

"Don't get upset. She's just drunk."

"Just drunk?" Wendy echoed incredulously. "How would you like your mother to be drunk when you introduced her to me?"

"I'll help you get her upstairs. Don't cry, Wendy. Please, don't cry."

She rubbed at her eyes and nose with the sleeve of her duffle coat, then grabbed one of Celia's arms.

"Come on!"

Celia emptied her glass and tossed it over her shoulder. It splintered against the fireplace and made Wendy cry out.

"Oh, Joe!"

They ran out to the hall with Celia staggering wildly between them. Then they struggled upstairs with her as quickly as possible. Once in the bedroom they flung her bodily on to the bed.

Coloured circles whirled violently around her.

Complete oblivion was approaching.

Chapter Twenty-two

Joe felt one of his headaches coming on. The embarrassment with Wendy's mother had been terrible and then Wendy was so upset she pleaded with him to stay the night. He did not want to leave her in the state she was in, especially as she would have to cope alone with her mother if Mrs King decided to get up again. Yet to sleep with Wendy under her parents' roof seemed so criminal it made him sweat.

Then there were his own parents.

It he got up early and hurried home first thing, and slipped in very quietly they might never find out that he had not come home the night before. It would just be his rotten luck though if his mum or dad looked into his room to check that he was there.

What could he say?

His father would kill him.

His mother would never let him live it down.

"I can't," he kept protesting to Wendy. "What if your mother woke up and came through. She'd get the police to me."

"No, that's the one thing she wouldn't do." Wendy clung to him and wept like a baby. "You don't know what she's like, Joe. She's all twisted and neurotic. She doesn't care what happens to me. Don't leave me, Joe."

He had been persuaded eventually and they lay in each other's arms stiffly listening until, exhausted, they dropped off to sleep.

The next day was Saturday, usually his favourite day, because he did not need to go to school. This was one Saturday however when he would have paid all the money in his Post Office Savings book to be allowed to spend the whole day at school. At least he would have been safe for a few hours.

There was no escape. If he stayed in Wendy's house her mother would catch him and probably have a fit.

His situation reminded him of a painting called "Between the Devil and the Deep Blue Sea".

In the morning he slipped away without breakfast and all the way home to tried to gather up his courage. He was, after all, nearly seventeen. In a little over a year from now he would be allowed by law to go into a pub and drink liquor. At that age, too, he would be liable for call-up if there were a war. So why should he not stay out all night if he wanted to?

He failed to convince himself. He knew too many reasons why his parents would regard what he had done as an unforgivable sin.

He was still only sixteen. Wendy was only fifteen. He had not phoned his parents. If they had been waiting for him coming home they would have had a long wait. It would not have improved their tempers.

There was also the fact that they had forbidden him to see Wendy.

Then it was a pity that Wendy was a Protestant. Not that he cared a tinker's cuss himself. Wendy was just Wendy and he was just Joe. They loved each other. It was as simple as that.

Only parents complicated everything.

He hoped they had both died during the night. It was not the first time he had envied orphans.

As soon as he opened the door, fury exploded in his face.

"Where the hell do you think you've been?" his father roared and covered the length of the lobby with huge rapid strides. Big paws clamped on Joe's collar and hauled him into the kitchen.

Joe struggled violently to shake himself free.

"Leave me alone, you big ape!"

"I'll 'big ape' you! Answer me! Where have you been? Your mother and I have been nearly demented all night."

"Oh, sure!" Joe's mouth twisted with bitter sarcasm. "I can imagine!"

"No, you cannot." His father thrust his face closer. "You obviously have neither imagination nor brains. You're a selfish, insensitive idiot!"

His mother took up the cry:

"Glory be to God, Joe, where have you been?"

Joe braced himself.

"At Wendy's house."

He might as well have dropped a bomb at their feet.

After a minute's shocked silence his mother said:

"Jesus, Mary and Joseph! What kind of parents has that girl got? They must be worse than her."

"Her father was away somewhere. I didn't want to leave Wendy on her own, that was all. She wasn't feeling well."

"Did you sleep with her?" his father asked.

"Yes."

Immediately his mother rushed forward and belted him across the face, one side after the other as if she had been saving up the energy for years.

"Dirty pup! Wicked rascal! That's a mortal sin! You go to confession! You do penance, do you hear?"

His father pushed her aside.

"What was the girl's mother doing all night?"

"Sleeping too, I suppose."

"Could you beat it?" Biddy gasped incredulously. "Her that's so toffee-nosed. Her that thinks she's such a lady. It's a disgrace!"

"I'll have something to say to her!" his father promised. "I'll have a word with her majesty as well."

"No, please don't cause any trouble." Joe's eyes widened with anxiety. "Mrs King didn't know anything about me sleeping with Wendy."

"It's you that's causing the trouble, lad. And you're liable to cause a lot more if you're not careful."

"Next he'll be telling us she's pregnant."

Joe's heart began to thump. He suddenly blurted out words as if they were too hot for his mouth.

"She is pregnant!"

"Glory be to God!" his mother wailed.

"You fool!" his father groaned. "You're only sixteen. What's to become of your life now? What about art school? What about your career?"

"Nothing's changed," Joe said.

His mother rolled her eyes heavenwards, turned away and lit up a cigarette.

"Nothing's changed, he says!"

"Do the girl's parents know?"

"That's why I went there last night."

"So you told Mrs King."

"No."

"Why not?"

"She was drunk."

His mother laughed incredulously.

"Drunk?"

Joe bristled. "You can take a bucket youself!"

Her hand whipped out and belted him again.

"Don't you dare accuse me of anything. I've been a good mother to you and don't you forget it. When I think of what I've sacrificed for you, and this is all the thanks I get . . ."

"Joe, what do you think you're going to do?" his father interrupted.

Joe shrugged. "Get married, I suppose."

His mother said, "You'll be lucky if you don't get the jail."

"Talk sense, lad. You couldn't keep yourself, never mind a wife. Anyway what do you think her parents are going to say? Do you think they're going to allow her to get married at her age?"

"They can't stop her once she's sixteen. It's Scottish law that once you're . . ."

"Don't you spout law to me, lad. I'm the magistrate around here. The fact remains she's only fifteen and still at school. Marriage is out of the question."

"But we love each other," Joe protested. "We want to get married."

"Oh, shut up!" His mother dismissed him, brushed him aside. "What do you know about love?" All her attention switched to her husband. "We'll have to talk this out before we go to Bearsden. I wouldn't have minded so much if it had been a Catholic girl from round here. Somebody with a nice family we could have been friendly with. If it had been somebody decent we could have all chipped in and given them a nice wedding and he could have got a job and they could have either lived with the girl's folks or here."

She tossed her cigarette into the fire. "But trust him to pick a bad 'un. She's maybe only fifteen but already she's been in trouble with the police and now this."

"It wasn't her fault," Joe said, but she ignored him and continued.

"And that bitch she's got for a mother. Can you see us ever being friendly with her? And from what I saw of the father he doesn't look the type we'd want to have anything to do with either."

"I don't want you to have anything to do with them," Joe said. "Just you keep out of it. It's none of your business."

His father's fist beat a tattoo against his shoulders.

"Less of your lip to your mother. You treat her with respect while you're under my roof. You thank God you've got a decent mother. In spite of all the cheek and ingratitude she's had to suffer from you, she's trying to help you. We're both trying to help you. So do as she says and shut up!"

"Charming!" Joe laughed sarcastically. "This is just great!"

"No, it's not great," his father shouted. "It's a damned disgrace and you ought to be ashamed of yourself. You've got somebody into trouble. No matter what she was like before, you're responsible for what she's like now."

"I'm not denying I'm responsible. I told you. I love Wendy and I want to marry her. I don't see what all the fuss is about."

"Well, you're a fool!" His father pushed the words close to his face.

Joe clutched at his courage.

"Well, so are you! I've seen Frank's birth certificate and your wedding certificate and I can count. You were older than me but you had a shotgun wedding!"

Immediately his father's hands shot out and grabbed him by the throat, but Joe had had enough.

Temper gave him the extra strength needed to wrench the hands away. Then he landed a punch on his father's chin that knocked his head back, and a belly blow that doubled him, gasping, forward.

His mother screamed and caught his father in her arms.

Joe ran.

Chapter Twenty-three

"What did you say on the phone!" Biddy asked.

"Just that I had to see her and I was coming straight over."

"What did she say to that?"

"Nothing. I never gave her the chance. I just hung up."

"Do I look all right?"

McGouran snatched his eyes from the road to give her a quick appraisal.

"Fine," he lied.

It was difficult to pinpoint exactly what was wrong with

Biddy. Maybe he was just too fussy. He had always been an extremely fastidious and conscientious man. That was why he was a good councillor and magistrate, a man above and beyond corruption, a man dedicated to good service and good order. Impossible to separate the public man from the private one. He needed good organisation in his home, too, and Biddy was so slap-happy and careless he often felt cornered and forced to over-react.

Long ago he had ceased to depend on her to have a shirt or clean handkerchief ironed ready if there was a meeting of the council or some occasion in connection with the City Chambers. He had learned, by trial and error, how to iron them himself.

Usually she bundled all the dirty wash into a bag and took it to the launderette every week so at least his clothes were clean.

Now he bought drip-dry shirts, and washed them himself. He made a pull-out bar over the bath on which to hang them on hangers until they were dry. Then he carefully folded them away in his drawer.

Biddy's carelessness soon littered over, however, and spoiled this arrangement. He would find stockings tossed over his shirts or underwear or blouses that left coloured stains.

He kept his trousers in a trouser press and his jackets on hangers, and always brushed his clothes and shoes meticulously before going out.

Biddy's clothes never looked smart unless they were brand new. She was always buying coats and dresses and shoes. For every occasion she had to have something. Yet still she never looked quite right.

One day he might be senior magistrate. One day he might even be Lord Provost of Glasgow. But it would be in spite of his wife, certainly not because of her.

The sight of her plump figure in one of her tight, bright dresses never failed to depress him. Nevertheless, sitting beside her in the car on their way to Bearsden, he was conscious of a certain affection radiating between them.

They had been married a long time and they believed in

the sacrament of marriage. Their recent troubles and worries had brought them together again physically. And there could be no denying that Biddy was good in bed. He had acquired a new sense of comfort and well-being. A sense of belonging and rightness too. It was good to be a part of a family and to know that he and his family were part of a bigger family of the Mother Church.

He likened it in a way to being in the forces during the war. It did not matter what kind of a person he was or where he happened to be, if he met someone else wearing the same uniform he experienced this recognition, this camaraderie, this sense of belonging.

"Anyway, she'd better not look down her nose at me," Biddy said. "I'll soon put her nose in a sling."

"You should have seen her face when I told her to mind her own business," McGouran laughed, remembering. "I told you I had lunch with her?"

"It's a wonder she managed to lower herself to be seen with you."

"She was ogling me as hard as she could."

"Rotten bitch!"

"You'd think Joe would have had more sense. Why the hell did he have to get mixed up with this lot?"

"That must be the house there."

He stopped the car and Biddy struggled out with a flash of bulging leg right up to her suspenders.

"Come on, Al," she urged from the pavement as she tugged the skirt of her purple suit down over her hips and tidied her white fabric gloves round her wrists.

The Kings' house seemed very quiet. In the distance the faint sound of traffic hummed like an electric saw, but the tree-lined garden was isolated by the chirping of birds and a continuous rustling of leaves.

He stabbed his finger against the doorbell.

"She'd better be in," he growled. "After me phoning."

She came running. He heard and wondered at the eager rush of feet. The door burst open and she stood breathless and bright-eyed. She was wearing a white flowing néglígé that looked stunning against her black hair and feverish scarlet face.

Her eyes fastened immediately, hungrily on him.

Holy Mother of God! She thought he had come to lay her!

He saw her notice Biddy then clutch at the lintel as if to prevent herself from collapsing.

"Well!" Biddy gasped. "If I hadn't seen it with my own eyes I wouldn't have believed it! Now we know who the randy schoolgirl takes after."

Mrs King's eyes darted anxiously past them. Her face had gone a sickly shade of grey.

"Come inside," she pleaded. "Someone might be listening! I . . . I . . . thought it was my husband."

"Pull the other leg," Biddy said. "It's got bells on it!"

Mrs King showed them into a luxurious sitting-room.

"Keep your voice down, please."

"Don't you tell me what to do, you bitch."

"That's enough, Biddy," McGouran interrupted. "We've things to talk about." He eased his big frame into a chair. "I suggest you pour youself a drink. I've news that might prove a shock."

Without a word she poured out three stiff whiskies, gave one to Biddy, one to him. Then she sank gracefully on to a chair nursing her own glass. He could see she was struggling desperately for calmness. Her nostrils slowly, deeply, sucked in air. Her chin tipped up.

Now that her face had lost its colour, she looked frail and ghost-like in the white négligé as if a sudden gust of wind might blow her completely away.

"You knew our Joe and your Wendy have been going out together. Well, now Joe tells us the girl's pregnant."

She stared at him with blank, shuttered eyes.

Biddy said, "I've no doubt there's been more than one of course. Joe's just getting the blame."

"Mrs King, did you hear what I said? Your daughter's pregnant."

"Oh, no!"

McGouran could not help feeling sorry for her. She

looked so bewildered and helpless. Then to his surprise she began to change into a picture of stark terror. A wet curtain of perspiration covered her face. Her eyes grew large and black and she trembled so much her whisky glass clattered on to the table. He refilled it for her, pressed it into her hands and helped her to lift the glass to her mouth.

"We would have waited until your husband returned but Joe ran out. We thought he might be here. He slept here last night."

Celia gazed imploringly up at him, whisky trickling from one corner of her mouth.

"Oh, no!"

"Oh, yes!" Biddy said. "While you were laid out, blind drunk!"

Mrs King closed her eyes.

"Leave off, Biddy. Getting her into a state isn't going to solve anything. Is Joe here, Mrs King?"

She shook her head.

"Where's the girl?" Biddy asked.

Again the head moved from side to side.

"I realise what a tragedy this must be for you," McGouran said gruffly. "You'll have your plans for your child just as I have for mine. But this has happened now and we've got to face facts." He sat down again. "Now, I'm willing to pay half of any expenses incurred in connection with the confinement. Any nursing-home expenses, cut them down the middle. After the birth, if you don't want to keep the baby my wife has offered to take it. She'll look after it as if it were her own. She can't do better than that."

"We're good Catholics," Biddy informed her. "Just in case you didn't know!"

Mrs King sipped quickly at the rest of her whisky, took a deep breath then sent words hurrying out as if she were reciting an exercise.

"You can both go away and forget all about this. There will be no baby. As far as you're concerned this unfortunate business is over. Just keep your son away from my daughter, that's all!"

"What do you mean—no baby?" Biddy cried out.

"Keep your voice down, please!"

"Never mind my voice. You explain to my man and me exactly what you mean."

"I told you it is no longer any concern of yours. Wendy is my daughter. I'll deal with her."

McGouran said, "It seems to me that you haven't been very successful in dealing with her so far, Mrs King."

"And don't you forget your daughter's carrying our son's child."

"You said yourself that it might not be his."

"Joe insists that he is responsible," McGouran said. "And I believe him. I think you'd better accept that your daughter is carrying our son's child. Now, I'd like an answer to my wife's question and I'm not leaving here until I get one."

"I'll arrange for an abortion, of course."

"Abortion!" Biddy shouted. "No, you will not!"

"Please, please, keep your voice down!"

"Oh, shut up!"

"Biddy, keep your head. Just calm down. Leave this to me. You heard us say we were good Catholics, Mrs King. We could never agree to what you suggest."

"I don't care what you are," Mrs King said.

"You'll have to care," Biddy interrupted, "whether you like it or not!"

"I don't care what you are," Mrs King repeated. "All I know is I cannot be involved in such a scandal."

Biddy gave a sarcastic laugh.

"Scandal, she says! What's abortion, may I ask?"

"That way, no one need ever know."

Biddy grimaced.

"You're a disgrace to the name of 'mother'. But you're not going to have our grandchild butchered. Even if it means that I've to look after your girl until her time's past."

Give credit where credit was due, McGouran told himself, Biddy had a heart as big as a bucket.

"Maryhill's only a stone's throw from here. Everybody would still get to know." Mrs King flapped her hands as if she were shooing away a flock of birds. "Just go away and keep your son away. I refuse to have anything more to do with any of you!"

Chapter Twenty-four

For quite a long time after she came home from the hospital Owen's name was never mentioned. She determined that Peter would never regret making him move to a flat of his own. To make herself attractive and desirable to him became an obsession. Often she bathed twice a day and sprayed herself with vaginal deodorants as well as the normal under-arm kind. She had to be absolutely sure she was fresh and fragrant so that she had no need to worry about Peter having an aversion to her for any reason connected with personal hygiene.

A lot of time was spent in front of the bedroom mirror putting on her make-up. Each eyelash was brushed and curled to perfection. She used a brush for her lips, too, so that there was a clear, well-shaped line.

And never had there been such a bedroom. It was a pink and white and gold dream with delicate touches of lavender and blue. Dresden figures adored each other along the top of the mantelpiece. Fragile gold filigree writhed into lovers' knots across the white furniture. Frilly fans and tasselled perfume sprays, huge fluffy powder-puffs, hairbrushes and hand-mirrors with embroidered backs cluttered the dressing-table.

Many anxious hours were spent in the bedroom preparing herself for Peter. Then every evening she busied herself in the kitchen making meals she knew he would enjoy. And every evening she greeted him with a smile and was ready to listen attentively to his news, or to sympathise with his problems.

They began to look up old school friends, and make up foursomes at bridge, and have an occasional dinner party.

Life was not idyllic, although it never failed to appear so

to outsiders. There were dark empty corners. There were moments of uncertainty and bewilderment. But on the whole she believed they were slowly and surely achieving something worthwhile. They were gathering shared experiences to bind them together. They were building, brick by brick, a good, stable, friendly relationship. They were creating their own little world.

She loved him.

Then one day she came home late from a shopping expedition. He was in the sitting-room reading a newspaper and sipping a Martini.

"Sorry I'm late, darling," she called on her way to the kitchen. "Won't be a jiffy. I've a salad already prepared."

Her voice was cheerful and normal although she sensed from the fleeting glimpse of Peter that something was wrong. His eyes were fixed on his newspaper but he was tensely concentrating on her. He was waiting and listening.

She saw the flowers immediately she entered the kitchen. They were carefully arranged in a tall vase on the table. Instinct told her they were from Owen and that Peter and Owen were testing her. This was a first step in a hopeful plan to worm Owen back into the house. Peter had not changed at all. The only person Peter really cared about was his friend. She felt the waiting silence reach out from the sitting-room and creep up her back. The intensity, the desperation of it was obscene.

In a moment Peter would stroll through, his every movement slowed down with affected casualness. He would expect her to cry out: "What gorgeous flowers!" or "Where did the lovely flowers come from?"

Then he would say, "Owen brought them for you. Nice of him, wasn't it?"

Peter strolled into the kitchen, whistling feebly.

She said nothing.

He wandered awkwardly around the room jingling coins in his trouser pockets.

She peeled off her gloves, lit a cigarette, placed dishes and cutlery on the trolley.

Sometimes they had their evening meal in the dining-room; sometimes, if they wanted to watch television, they ate at a little table beside the fire in the sitting-room. Tonight she wanted to watch television. She hoped it would hypnotise her, blot out her thoughts.

The pleasant, affectionate, happy life she and Peter had been sharing disappeared like a mirage that had never had any substance. Reality was the nightmare, after all.

She hardly knew what she was doing. The salad bowl, the biscuits and cheese, the cream and sugar materialised from nowhere on to the trolley. The coffee filled the pot. She walked around clicking doors and reaching up to shelves.

She was alone in a cold place and from far off, as if she were looking from another planet down to earth, she could see with her mind's eye all over Bearsden, inside cosy yellow-windowed villas other women serving meals to their husbands. Old women, young women, fat women, thin women, good-natured women, bad-tempered women, pretty women, plain women. It did not seem to matter what other women were like, their husbands loved them.

What terrible thing was it about her that made it impossible for Peter to feel like that? How did she cause the aversion that she tried not to see but knew was always there? Her inward eye sought to examine herself but kept reeling away from a crumbling corpse she could not recognise.

"Everything's ready," she told Peter. "Will you take the trolley through to the sitting-room while I run upstairs to powder my nose?"

Returning downstairs the first thing she noticed in the sitting-room was the vase of flowers. Peter had surreptitiously brought them through and placed them on the centre of the mantelpiece. There was no escaping the charade.

"Where did the flowers come from?" she asked.

There was an immediate transformation in Peter. In a flash he was all eagerness. His eyes sparkled. He rubbed his hands.

"Owen brought them for you. Wasn't that kind of him?

He dropped in earlier for a cup of tea. He misses the old place."

"Oh?" She raised an eyebrow and stared at him with cool knowledgeable eyes. "What do you want with your salad? Meat or fish?"

He paused uncertainly, his eyes dodging hers.

"Fish."

She lived for time's healing hands to blot out the incident. Another night, another day, another rubber of bridge, another dinner party. How they chattered at times. What long silences could drop between them. Life was time. A passage of endurance, a marking time between birth and death.

She felt Owen's presence on Peter. She saw Owen in Peter's eyes.

She tried to tell herself that everything was perfectly natural. Owen was, after all, Peter's business partner and his best friend. She saw what outsiders could see. What a lucky couple they were. They had money. They had a lovely home. Her husband was charming and attentive. He had even agreed at last that she should have a child. She was so grateful she clung to him and wept unashamedly.

During her pregnancy he had insisted that she went to London for a holiday and to buy new outfits.

"There are no really fashionable maternity clothes in Glasgow, Celia. Have a trip to London. Stay as long as you like. Enjoy yourself and buy some really smart things."

Then, after the birth when she had come home from the hospital, Mrs Anderson had said:

"Wasn't it nice of your husband's partner to come and stay with him and keep him company while you were away? It was so nice to see him at the church again, too."

The spare bed in Peter's room had been slept in. The coverlet had been carefully smoothed up but underneath the sheets were crushed and the pillow showed a dark patch of grease.

She was not allowed to sleep here. In the same room as her husband. In her own house.

In sudden hysterical rage she ripped the bedclothes off the bed and flung them across the floor. Her nails clawed at the pillow-case and tore it to shreds. All the time she screamed against her teeth so that no one would hear. But as if sensing her distress the newborn baby cried out in panic from the other room. She ran to comfort and reassure it but could not lift it into her arms she was so distraught.

Weeping helplessly along with the child, she hated Owen as she had never hated him before. How could he take Peter away from her when now he was needed all the more? How could Peter bring Owen into her home when he knew it would upset her?

The situation seemed to go against all the laws of nature. She had a newborn baby and herself to look after. She felt the need to protect herself and her child against two hostile men. She did not feel safe.

Their world belonged to Peter and Owen. She would always be out in the cold struggling to protect herself or fighting futilely to get in. She felt inadequate and confused and when Peter returned home from work the baby was screaming, the house was a shambles, there was no food ready and she was wandering aimlessly about.

He greeted the scene with cheerful relief. He laughed. It was strange and frightening to watch his happiness when she was ill.

After he had shut her away in her quiet frilly room he went about the house whistling. She kept the baby beside her in bed and lay anxiously listening. Sometimes she thought she heard male voices coming from downstairs and eventually she asked Peter if anyone was there. He told her it was Owen.

"Not staying here? Not again?" Her voice raised like a hand warding off fear.

"Darling," Peter soothed, "it's only for a little visit. He's going back to the flat, I promise. You surely can't object to an occasional visit. After all, poor Owen's got nobody but me. You've got the baby!"

The baby began to wail and then scream. Scream and

scream and echo deep, deep echo, echo down long tunnels of mind and soul and endless anguished years.

Chapter Twenty-five

Wendy knew Joe had arranged previously to meet the boys. She was not to see him until evening. But he felt so much a part of her now she could not wait. Without him she was incomplete, waiting in suspense, dangling in nothingness.

Already her mother had spoiled their happiness and they had not yet told her about the baby.

She felt uncertain and insecure.

Shame brought misery and scorching heat to her face and pulled down her eyes. Her mother had kept wriggling provocatively and dancing round and round Joe, and looking at him, and touching him, like a one-scene film repeating itself over and over again.

She felt frightened. Strange, half-formed anxieties flicked around her with the speed of shadows and could not be recognised.

She had been half-asleep when Joe went away and she had never even said "cheerio".

Apprehension shook her wide awake. What if Joe died and she had not said goodbye?

She scrambled from the bed to tug on a jersey and a pair of jeans. Then, not caring if her mother heard her, she ran, feet thumping rapidly, downstairs.

The house still slept. Her fingers, clumsy with speed, dialled Joe's number.

"Joe? Is that you, Joe?"

"McGouran speaking."

Her heart pattered high in her throat.

"Is Joe there, please? I must speak to Joe. It's important."

"No doubt. But he's not here. I've no idea where he's run off to."

Both Wendy's hands clutched at the receiver as if it were holding her up.

"Run off?"

"That's what I said. Now bring your mother to the phone. I want to talk to her."

"What about?"

"You know very well what about."

"Joe and I are going to speak to her."

"Get your mother to the phone."

"I don't want you to speak to her."

"Never mind what you want, just you do as you're told."

She dropped the receiver back. She wondered fearfully if her mother had heard it on the bedside extension.

McGouran would ring again at any minute.

To be alone when her mother found out was impossible. Shadows puffed up to giant size.

The telephone rang. She grabbed her duffle coat and flew from the house.

Her hair was uncombed. A frizzy red halo dwarfed her small face, still dazed with sleep.

She did not know where to go. "Joe ran off," she kept thinking. "Joe ran off?"

She found herself at Bearsden Cross. Her green gaze strafed the Saturday shoppers, the chattering women, the men waiting, arms hugging at boxes of groceries, the pert children, the pink babies in prams. Then she retreated to the café and reached it without being conscious of how she got there.

There were no familiar faces among the people sitting at the tables sipping coffee and spooning ice-cream.

She stared and stared as if, by sheer desperation, she could make Joe materialise. People were mere ghosts, wraiths, mists to penetrate in order to see Joe.

She wandered along towards Canniesburn Toll, not realising in which direction she was heading yet instinctively drawn towards where Joe lived in Maryhill.

She could have taken a bus from Canniesburn but she had no money with her and had to walk the long open stretch of Maryhill Road before reaching the first of the tenement houses past the park.

A sharp wind danced along and threw rain in her face and tugged back the hood of her duffle coat. Her hair darkened with damp and lay plastered close to her head.

She felt alone in a foreign land. Although Maryhill was so near Bearsden she had only passed quickly through it a few times on the way into town. The more usual route was along Great Western Road.

She crossed Maryhill Road at the Catholic church. Even from the outside it seemed an alien place with its strange shape and huge mural dominating the front wall. The Church of the Immaculate Conception. Even the name was strange. In Bearsden the churches she knew had solid, familiar geographical names like New Kilpatrick Church, or North Church, or South Church.

What did the Immaculate Conception mean?

The fear that had sent her running from the house settled on her shoulders like the cloak on the Virgin Mary of the painted wall.

Here the houses were different, the people were different, even the pavement under her feet had a different feel.

As she turrned into Seldon Street she passed two girls. They gave her piercing, hostile looks. They knew she was a stranger to their territory.

Joe's close was clean and quiet but her feeling of strangeness persisted. Even the name on Joe's door—McGouran—seemed tarred with the same brush.

She rang the bell and stood twisting at the toggles of her duffle coat and listening to the pounding of her heart.

After a minute or two, she again put a tentative finger on the bell. Again the house echoed with emptiness.

She stood for a long time in the close, praying that Joe would come, until eventually a car drew up outside. The bang of the car door made her twitch nervously.

Mr and Mrs McGouran had left the car and were coming towards her.

"Oh, you're there, are you!" McGouran growled. "We've just come from your place."

Wendy hastily stepped into protective armour.

"Oh?" She raised an eyebrow. "Had a good time, did you?"

McGouran opened the door with a key and jerked a thumb to indicate that she was to go inside.

Mrs McGouran said, "Impertinent monkey! What Joe saw in you I'll never know."

As they walked along the lobby Wendy's eyes strayed into one of the rooms, the door of which lay open. She saw pictures of sad-eyed Jesus, and the Cross, and a saintly-looking Mary. The sombre-coloured paintings had a peculiar old-fashioned look like the statues sitting on the dresser beneath them.

In the sitting-room, McGouran came straight to the point.

"Your mother's determined to arrange for an abortion right away but it'll be over our dead bodies. We're not going to allow any butcher to murder our grandchild."

"And it doesn't matter what you say . . ." Mrs McGouran began but Wendy interrupted.

"I don't know what you're talking about."

Biddy was shaking with indignation as she lit a cigarette.

"We're talking about your mother going to pay to sneak you into a private place in town so that some man who's a disgrace to the name of doctor can stick a knife in you and kill that poor innocent baby."

Wendy heard herself say, "I won't let her. Where's Joe?"

Mr McGouran shrugged.

"Your guess is as good as mine. But he'll be back. I'll tell him to phone you."

"Keep her here, Al! There's no telling what that bitch in Bearsden's liable to get up to. She's probably been on the phone and got the whole thing arranged already."

"Yes, I'll just stay here and wait for Joe."

"No," McGouran said firmly. "God alone knows when he'll put in an appearance. It could be the middle of the night. By that time your mother would have the police out searching for you."

"I don't care!"

"Well, I do! I'll phone and tell your mother to come and collect you."

"No need," she tossed her head. " I know the way!"

How she got out of the house she would never know. She kept seeing a man poised over her with a long knife.

She walked home like a mechanical doll, staring straight ahead.

Her mother was waiting for her. She was sitting on the edge of a chair with a whisky glass in one hand and a cigarette in the other. Her jar of librium capsules was on a coffee table next to the chair. The pupils of her eyes were black discs that blotted out colour. She was swaying a little.

"You wicked, wicked girl! How could you do this to me?"

"I haven't done anything to you. It's you who are trying to do something to me. The McGourans told me."

"The McGourans!" Her mother's face creased with pain and she closed her eyes. "Even the name! Wendy, how could you?"

"How could I what?"

"It's not that I mind the man being a socialist. It's not that I mind them being Catholics. Some of my best friends are Catholics. But the McGourans are so dreadful. They came here bullying and raising their voices and behaving in a most ignorant and shocking manner. One only needs to look at the mother . . ."

"I don't care about them. All I care about is Joe."

Chapter Twenty-six

"Please, oh, please!" Celia moaned. "Just let's get it over with. Quietly, discreetly, without any more fuss or talk."

"By all means!" Peter flung out his arms and rumpled his fingers through his hair and paced rapidly up and down. "But can you blame me for getting upset when this is what meets me the moment I arrive home? Honestly, Celia, that girl gets on my wick. She really is dreadful. I don't know what I've done to deserve this. I work my fingers to the bone for the pair of you. I provide you with this gorgeous home and everything you fancy . . ."

"You'd think it was all my fault to hear you talk. She's your child as well as mine. And no one can say I haven't been a good mother. I've never once raised my voice to Wendy. I've been nothing but patient and considerate and kind to her."

"I'm not saying it's your fault." He rolled his eyes. "My God, I don't know what I'm saying. All my life I've been respectable and respected."

"No one's going to know anything about it, Peter. I've arranged everything."

She knew she could not depend on him. It was always the same. Either he was not here when she needed him or, if he was, he couldn't cope.

The only place he could function efficiently was at his job. He was an excellent hair stylist. In his salon his fingers flicked and fluttered with amazing expertise. He angled mirrors at customers and pattered enthusiastically.

"You look gorgeous, dear, simply gorgeous! Didn't I tell you I was clever?"

Everyone vied for his attention. They all enjoyed a good gossip and laugh and each customer liked to think that she was his favourite and he was her special confidant and friend.

"Will she keep her mouth shut, though? You know what she's like."

"I've warned her. I've threatened everything I can think of. I've tried to explain we're only thinking of her own good."

"And what about this dreadful gangster she's been going around with?"

"He phoned on Saturday night but luckily I'd already given Wendy one of my sleeping tablets and it knocked her out cold. I told him Wendy did not wish anything more to do with him and he must not phone again or make any attempts to contact her. But he phoned again on Sunday morning. Fortunately she was still sleeping so I repeated what I'd said. His father phoned as well. I told him I had nothing to say to him and that you would contact him as soon as you returned."

Peter began pacing the floor again.

"Why did you have to say that? I don't want to see any of them."

"I was only playing for time. I'd spoken to the doctor in Glasgow and he was trying to arrange a bed for Wendy right away."

"And a pretty penny he's charging for it!"

She gave a sigh.

"I'd gladly give everything I owned to have this awful business over and done with so that we can forget all about it once and for all."

"I know! I know! But honestly, Celia, doesn't it get on your wick! Does she know she's going today?"

"I thought it ould save any long arguments and fuss if we left it to the last minute. I suppose I'd better get her downstairs now. She's been lying on top of her bed like a zombie, refusing to eat anything, not saying a word."

"Shall I call her?"

"She'll just ignore you."

"Charming!"

"We'd better both go up and explain."

"You already have explained, you said."

"I want to make sure she understands it's for her own good."

It reminded Celia of the time when she had to face the ordeal of going to court. As she climbed the stairs to her daughter's room she prayed for time to pass quickly so that this new and terrifying episode would fade into the distant past.

The child still lay, fully clothed, on top of the bed, a startling contrast of white skin, brown freckles and bright red hair.

"Come on, darling," Celia said gently. "We're ready."

Emerald eyes swivelled towards her.

"Ready for what?"

"Your little visit to the nursing home. It'll only take a day or two and you won't feel a thing."

The child shrunk up, slid back.

"I'm not going!"

'Daddy and I are going with you, dear. We'll be there all the time. You'll be perfectly all right."

"I'm not going!"

"There's nothing to be afraid of. We promise."

"I'm not going!"

"Now look here, m'lady . . ." her father burst out impatiently. "You've caused us enough trouble and worry. You've got to go so stop making things even more difficult and distressing. Have some consideration!"

"Go away and leave me alone!"

"Please, Wendy," her mother pleaded. "Can't you understand? You've no choice, darling. You're only a child. You're still at school. You've only just sat your 'O' levels. You've your Highers to start studying for now. Then there's art school. That's what you've always wanted, isn't it?"

"Yes."

"Well, then."

She took Wendy's coat from the wardrobe and held it out.

"I've already packed your nighty and toilet things in my nice weekend case. It's downstairs ready in the hall."

"No Mummy, please. I'm frightened."

"Darling!"

Celia eased her from the bed until she was standing cradled close in her arms.

"It's going to be all right. I told you. Now get this coat on. There's a good girl."

Peter hurried forward and helped Celia to manoeuvre Wendy into the coat.

"It'll be all right," Celia kept murmuring. "It'll soon be all over and you'll be able to forget all about it. The whole dreadful business will be a thing of the past."

Suddenly Wendy pushed them both away.

"It wasn't a dreadful business until you made it dreadful. Joe and I were happy. We wanted the baby. I still do!"

"Don't be ridiculous!" Her father glanced at his wrist-watch. "It's time we had her out of here. Come on now, we've had enough of your nonsense, m'lady. You're coming whether you like it or not!"

They took an arm each, held on firmly and propelled the child towards the door.

Celia began to feel sick with distress as Wendy dragged back with all her weight, trembling violently.

"No, Mummy. Mummy, please, oh, please, Mummy!"

Peter said:

"This is ghastly. I can see me having to knock her out."

Wendy kept frantically appealing to her mother.

"Mummy, Mummy, Mummy!"

A stab of unbearable pain let loose years of pent-up frustration before Celia had time to summon yoga or anything else to her aid.

"Shut up! Shut up!" She dug her nails into Wendy's arm and shook her with such violence that Wendy battered against Peter and shock dazed her face. "You selfish, demanding, blood-sucking little brat. I can't cope anymore. I've had enough. Don't you understand? Can't you see past your own sordid little affairs? I'm ill. Do you hear? I'm ill! I'm not fit to put up with you any more!"

Wendy began to cry. It was dreadful sound, jerky, high-pitched moans of terror. She sounded like a trapped animal.

It was wicked of her to make such sounds.

They were only trying to help her. They were only thinking of her own good.

Again they pulled her towards the door but this time she let out a scream.

Peter immediately clamped his hand over her mouth.

"My God, Celia!" he said. "What are we going to do?" Celia was trembling now.

"Wendy," she said quietly. "If you do that again and the neighbours hear you, you will have something to be afraid of. Daddy and I will kill you!"

Slowly Peter lowered his hand from Wendy's mouth. The child was jerking and tottering like an old woman.

"I . . . I . . . don't feel very well, Mummy. Honestly,

Mummy. I . . . I . . . cou . . . couldn't walk out to the car. I'm sorry, Mu . . . Mummy, I'll go tomorrow, I promise. I'll be a good girl tomorrow, Mummy. I promise. Just let me go back to my own bed just now. Please . . . Mummy, oh, please."

Peter said:

"Maybe you'd better phone."

Another night, Celia thought, another night of suspense and agony. She rubbed a hand over her eyes.

"It's your own fault, you know, Wendy. You brought this upon yourself. We're only trying to help you. We're older than you and we know what's best."

"Yes, Mummy!"

"You promise you'll go quietly and not indulge in any of this shocking behaviour tomorrow?"

Saucer-eyed, Wendy nodded.

"Well, have a little rest just now while I go downstairs and make something nice for lunch. You'll feel much better after you've had something nourishing to eat."

"Owen's had to take on some of my clients as well as his own today because of all this," Peter complained. "He'll be harassed off his feet. It's a damned shame!"

Outside Wendy's door Celia put her hand over her eyes again.

She breathed slowly, rhythmically, deeply, and tried not to listen to the little animal noises.

Chapter Twenty-seven

There were two car parks at Bearsden Cross, one behind the shops at Roman Road and another tucked away down at the end of Kirk Road. The latter used to be a field belonging to the manse before the council took it over.

The Bearsden crowd had been resentful and angry at first.

"There's going to be no place left for us to have a decent game of football," they grumbled.

But it had turned out fine. The field had certainly been concreted over but the winding burn had been left to gurgle and splash alongside and the high green banks still rustled with bushes and bowing trees.

Gash Merrilees brought a ball, a big, firm, bouncy white one and they all descended on the car park and filled it to high heaven with lusty shouting and throaty roars of laughter.

They always clattered and leapt and bounced high with the ball, heading it and kicking it between each other until they reached the far end. The entrance part was of uneven shape but at the far end there was a good big oblong part just perfect for a pitch.

They set up the goal areas, two bricks for each goal.

Those with the longest hair like Gash and Joe tugged their school ties from their necks and fixed them round their heads, Indian style.

It was a five-a-side match. They all wore tight, faded denims and sandshoes and their shirts hung out, flapping loosely.

Joe felt exhilarated as he raced after the ball and bounded high in the air to feel the thump and jar of it against his head. He enjoyed running circles round everyone with the ball at his feet.

The air reverberated with yells.

"Out on the wing."

"Cross it!"

"You duffed it! That was an easy ball!"

"Again!"

"Watch your back!"

"You're on your own!"

He slammed the ball into the goal.

He started out on the touch-line and beat Gash Merrilees and wham —the ball shot past Spiro MacLean.

He felt as if he had springs on his heels, and muscles like rocks on his legs, and great glorious lungs like bellows.

It was good to be alive. It was good to be an artist and

alive. Even as he rushed about and yelled with the others, he was still aware of the trees holding up the sky, and the purple and blue and green rainbow patches lapping on the water, and the glossy texture and subtle shading of each blade of grass.

He caught the scene and framed it—the trees, the river, his friends. He organised everything as a composition. Line and movement were painted on his mind with a brush of excitement.

After the game they were all ravenously hungry and split up to belt home for tea.

"How about coming up to see my new guitar, Beef?" Spiro invited. "You can get something to eat at my place and we can have a practice."

"Yeah, thanks." Joe accepted with enthusiasm and gratitude. Spiro was a real pal. Whenever he could manage a spare minute or two he gave him a lesson on the guitar. Spiro's folks were loaded with money. He went to a fee-paying school and his parents also paid for private music lessons.

His new guitar turned out to be an electric one. Joe was speechless with admiration.

"You can have my old one. Then you can practise as much as you like at home."

"For keeps, you mean?" Joe gasped, unable to believe his incredible good fortune.

"Yes. Maybe one day we could form a group, Beef."

"And make a disc?" Joe's eyes glazed. "And have our picture on the sleeve, the whole crowd of us, in real spanking gear."

"All posing round me on the bike gripping the ape-hangers." Spiro began to shout with excitement. "And you straddling the back!" '

"Yeah! We could wear denim jackets with the sleeves ripped off and nothing underneath."

"And old denim trousers, and rings on each hand."

"And a Saint Christopher round our necks on a fine gold chain."

"And bare feet."

"Oh great!"

It was one of the best days in his life and afterwards, plodding along Maryhill Road with Spiro's old guitar on his back, he whistled happily.

His father and mother pounced on him the moment he set foot in the house.

"Where have you been, you selfish hooligan?"

"Glory be to God, he's got a guitar now. That's all he needs!"

"Look, lad, you've caused your mother and me enough worry and trouble. It's time you grew up and acted like a man instead of a long-haired idiot!"

"What have I done now?" Joe shouted indignantly. "You're always picking on me."

"What have you not done, you fool!" his father bawled back. "You're fit for nothing. You'll never do anything. You'll never achieve anything. You'll never get anywhere. I don't suppose you've ever given your mother or me a thought but she has nightmares about you not going to church. And I'm ashamed when I hear my colleagues on the bench complain about all the long-haired louts they have to deal with. I know I've got one of my own at home."

His eyes bulged with anger.

"What have you done?" He began prodding Joe with a stiff poker finger. "I'll tell you what you've done, you ungrateful good-for-nothing hound. You've let us down. You've given us a showing up. You've been had up in court. You've got a girl into trouble."

His mother butted in.

"You've been away the whole day enjoying yourself while your dad and I have been getting into a terrible state. We've been to see that bitch in Bearsden and her daughter's been here looking for you. That bitch is trying to get an abortion arranged and where were you when all this was going on? Pinging away at that guitar, I suppose." As she lit a cigarette she turned, puffing smoke to her husband. "It's an atomic war we need to get rid of the whole, dirty, long-haired guitar-playing crowd of them!"

"You make me sick!" Joe said.

"You get to that phone," his father commanded, "and phone that girl!"

Joe's face hardened into a sneer. He raised an eyebrow.

"OK. OK. Keep your shirt on."

He nonchalantly dialled Wendy's number and was taken aback when her mother answered. She told him Wendy did not want to speak to him or have anything more to do with him and he must not contact her again.

He could not believe it. Yet he felt shaken.

Next morning, he phoned again and the same thing happened.

It was Sunday morning and if he had not arranged to meet Wendy in the morning to go sketching, they usually saw each other at the café.

He went there as soon as he could. There was no sign of her. He waited and waited.

The crowd was there and they drank coffee and ate chocolate cream snowballs and played games. But even during the games, when he was racing round the block, for instance, and trying to beat it back into the café within the prearranged time, Wendy still pulled at his attention and made him fling desperate glances around to see if she was coming.

She never came.

He plucked up courage and trudged along the road and up the path to her house and rang the doorbell.

Her father came, opened the door a crack, peered out with one eye and wailed that if he did not go away he would call the police. Then the door clicked shut.

It occurred to Joe that it was true what Wendy said. Her father was a poof.

He remained standing on the doorstep, big-shouldered arms dangling, trying to make up his mind what to do next.

Eventually he turned away.

Tomorrow he would go to the Academy and see Wendy there.

Next day he waited at the school gate from before three o'clock, just in case they happened to get away early.

Time dragged on. Pupils surged past him. Still no Wendy.

He caught sight of someone in her class and eagerly called out.

"Hey, seen Wendy?"

"No, she was absent today!"

He slouched home.

His father growled.

"Right! She said her husband would contact me as soon as he returned. I'll give him until tomorrow. If he hasn't phoned me by tomorrow night, after I come home from work, your mother and I are back there again."

"What about me?" Joe queried anxiously.

"You just shut up!" said his mother, and took herself off to bingo.

Soon afterwards his father squeezed his big body into a clean shirt, fixed his tie with great care in front of the mirror and slowly, meticulously brushed his hair and his suit. Then he swaggered round to the Ram's Head to meet his mates and argue over a pint about politics and what was wrong with the world.

Left alone in the house Joe sloped restlessly from room to room, shoulders hunched, hands dug deep into the front pockets of his denims.

The phone rang and suddenly Wendy's voice was gabbling, whispering, climbing high with hysteria.

"Oh, Joe, Joe, help me, oh, please. Take me away from here. Right away, tonight. Oh, quick, Joe, quick, promise you will, before anyone comes. I'm in Mummy's room at the extension. They might hear downstairs."

"Bring you over here, you mean?"

"No, no! They'd only come and get me again. Take me away, far away, Joe. We'll run away together. I'll meet you tonight after midnight at the Cross. You bring your rucksack and all your camping gear. I'll bring everything I need. I'll have to hang up now, Joe. I'm frightened."

He stood with the receiver still in his hand for a long time. Then slowly he replaced it and went through to his bedroom.

The walls were covered in sketches in black and white and colour. There was Charlie Brown. There was Linus sucking his thumb and clutching his blanket. There was Snoopy the flap-eared dog.

There was Chairman Mao and Martin Luther King and Ché Guevara. There was Pele in action.

Joe burst into tears. He wanted to go to art school. It was all arranged.

Wendy would be all right. Her folks would look after her. She would get over it.

Then one day, later on, when they were older and he had saved up enough money, they would get married.

He knew he was already thinking as if he were older.

It seemed to him that once you grew up you stopped thinking straight.

And the higher you grew the worse you became.

Heads of state used words like "containment" and "operation clean-up" when they meant shooting the blood and guts out of men, women and children.

Wendy was not all right.

He reached for his rucksack and began stuffing and punching his camping things into it. Then he hid the rucksack underneath the bed, and waited.

Darkness came slowly. The clock ticked his youth away.

His parents' bed creaked and creaked, then was silent.

He heaved up and hitched on the heavy rucksack and left the house.

Wendy was at the Cross. She looked very small.

His face sagged with shock and he felt frightened. For the first time he saw that she was only a little girl.

Her eyes searched his face.

"I just ran out. I've got nothing, Joe."

He hooked an arm around her shoulders.

"Come on!" he managed. "I've got enough for both of us!"

Chapter Twenty-eight

Empty room. Long, narrow, cam-ceiled, small-windowed like a cell. On the chest of drawers a doll, cracked-faced, one-eyed; sagging, brown, bald head low, legs splayed. A teddy bear, nose high, stiff-backed, stiff-armed, stiff-legged. Wardrobe door open. Wendy's duffle coat gone.

"Wendy?" Celia turned, calling.

She went to the bathroom and rattled at the handle of the locked door.

"Wendy?"

"For God's sake!" Peter's voice muffled through. "I'm in here."

Her own bedroom displayed itself like a beautiful confection.

Peter's room, brown and white, with two single beds. Characterless, as if even fingerprints had been carefully erased. Nothing had changed since Owen had stayed.

Dining-room waiting with breakfast laid. Shiny black pottery on orange linen. The sitting-room silent. Except for the clock tossing endless echoes through stale whisky and tobacco air. Kitchen busy with kettle boiling.

Automatically Celia made a pot of tea. She was still standing beside the cooker when Peter came in.

"Celia, I never slept a wink last night, did you? It was absolutely hellish."

"Wendy's gone."

"Gone? To the nursing home?"

"I would have thought that would be the last place. Remember yesterday?"

"I've been trying all night to forget. So, it was just a sneaky trick!" He flopped down at the kitchen table and propped up his brow with his hand. "That'll teach us not to trust her. 'I promise! I promise, Mummy!' she says. Honestly, Celia, she's the limit!"

"I wonder if she's gone to that boy's place."

"Oh yes. Our home isn't good enough for her. We're not good enough for her. She prefers to be with that young ape and live in a slum in Maryhill. Can you beat it? I just cannot understand that girl, can you? Now I've got a thumping headache."

"Peter, you'd better phone the McGourans."

"What good will that do? They're not going to help get Wendy to the nursing home, are they?"

"Just to see."

"They won't, I'm telling you."

"To see if she's there."

"Oh, all right, all right."

She followed him through to the phone, her face stiff, her eyes staring.

Peter protested and complained to himself as he dialled. "That girl had everything. I've worked and slaved to keep a respectable roof over her head. Nothing has ever been denied her. I've been as good a father as I know how to that girl and this all the thanks I get . . . Hello? . . . Oh, Mrs McGouran. This is Mr King, Wendy's father. Is Wendy there? . . . There's no need to be impertinent, Mrs McGouran. I only asked a civil question . . . Oh, my God! . . . Well, how was I to know that your son had . . . Well, yes, I suppose so . . . But it's not my fault, is it . . . Look here, if anyone's to blame it's your son . . . Well what are you and your husband going to do about it . . . Oh, well, if that's your attitude . . ." He flung down the receiver. "Common as dirt that woman. You should have heard the language of her."

Celia's eyes remained glued to his face.

"What's happened?"

"You might know! The pair of them are away together. Did you ever in all your life hear of anything so irresponsible and ridiculous?" He returned to the kitchen.

Celia said, "They can't have gone far. If we took the car and . . ."

"You must be joking!" he interrupted with a howl of derision. "We haven't a clue in which direction they went. You can't expect me to drive around endlessly through every street and back alley in the country. I'm fit for nothing as it is after all that carry on yesterday, and then not getting a wink of sleep. After a couple of aspirins and a cup of tea I'll have to phone Owen. I just couldn't face the rush in the salon today. I'm going back to bed. This has put me right off my stroke. I might as well go to bed. I'd just make a mess of every head I touched. Where are the aspirins?" Impatiently he jerked drawers open and shut.

"Never mind the aspirins just now. We've got to do something about Wendy."

"Oh, charming! It's a different story when you feel ill though."

"We can't just let them disappear. She's only fifteen and she's pregnant."

"Wendy is her boyfriend's responsibility now. We've done what we could. We've offered to do more, to put everything right for her. But she doesn't want to know, does she? If you fancy another struggle like yesterday, Celia, I certainly don't. They want to get married. Well, let them. Serves them right. That's all I've to say."

"I can't just stand here and do nothing. I wonder what the boy's father is saying. He spoke about his son's career. It seemed important to him. He'll surely want to try his best to find him."

"His wife said: 'The best of British luck to them!' Quite cheerful and spiteful she sounded."

"If only I could drive."

"Well, you can't."

"I'll speak to him."

"McGouran? You're wasting your time, Celia."

"He's got a car. I must do something," she repeated distractedly. "I don't care if we take all day and all night."

Peter's anger eased gently away. He gave a long sigh.

"If it wasn't for this devilish headache, I'd come too. But I really do feel rotten."

"Oh, dear, and I haven't even prepared anything for you to eat."

"I'll be all right. Don't worry."

His hand touched her shoulder and immediately she twisted her head round and kissed it with passionate gratitude.

Shrinking and wriggling, his fingers smeared lipstick grotesquely across her cheek and nose as they retreated.

"Off you go, love," he murmured.

The word "love" rocked her off balance. She gazed up at him with surprised, vulnerable eyes and sagging mouth. She could have dropped on her knees with gratitude. She would have done anything, anything for him. It was only with an agonising effort of will that she quietened her emotions. She nodded and without a word left him and went upstairs.

She forced herself to go through the calm familiar motions of powdering her face and brushing her hair and of choosing which coat and matching shoes and gloves to put on. Then without calling goodbye, in case he was already in bed and sleeping, she left the house, easing the door shut slowly and silently behind her.

"Good morning, Mrs King." The quick sharp cry came from the porch of the next villa. "You are early on the go today!" Mrs Anderson was clutching a couple of milk bottles to her chest. "Nothing wrong, I hope?"

Celia gave a little sideways tilt to her head and a charming smile as she passed.

"No, no. Lovely fresh morning, isn't it?"

It had been raining during the night and the pavements and trees of Bearsden glimmered with moisture. A thick earthy smell seduced her nostrils. She sucked it in and savoured it, despite the quickening panic in her gut.

She wanted to run, but she kept on walking, nostrils pinching in the pungent aromatic air.

Everywhere in Bearsden people were enacting safe, methodical, respectable routines. Coffee mornings were being prepared for. School uniforms were being donned. Cars were nosing from garages. Bowler hats and *Glasgow Heralds* were floating towards the city.

She took the train because she could get off at Queen Street Station which led on to George Square. There, approaching the City Chambers, her panic increased and whipped her mind into confusion and uncertainty. Suddenly she had no idea how McGouran would receive her. Thoughts of him made her feel so agitated she found herself walking past the entrance. She stopped a few yards away from the revolving doors, then returned to push her way through them.

"I'd like to see Bailie McGouran," she heard herself tell the council officer and she was more confused than ever by his reply.

"I'm sorry, madam. Bailie McGouran has gone to a conference in Aberdeen. He isn't due back in Glasgow until tomorrow."

The man had small, shrewd eyes. She avoided them.

Yes, she was feeling all right. Perfectly all right. No, it didn't matter. No, she did not wish to leave her name. No, no one else would do.

Out in the Square again, she gazed helplessly around. She clutched her handbag in front of her as if it were all she had to depend on to hold her up while statues, aloof on pedestals, gazed with stony disinterest over her head.

She went back to the station. To return home by the next train seemed the only safe thing to do.

She swallowed black coffee in the station buffet. She bought a magazine at the station bookstall. She flipped unseeingly through it, then rolled it up and gripped it tightly. She paced the platform, timing short steps with quick raps of book against fist.

She would snatch a few drinks as soon as she got home. A few drinks would calm her. Then she would talk to Peter again. They had to discuss what was to be done about Wendy.

The train scooped her up and hurried her away from the dusty clamour of the station and spilled her out once more into the dewy lushness of Bearsden. She prayed that Mrs Anderson would not see her. Holding her breath she moved as quietly as possible up the garden path. The key turned silently in the lock. Inside. Safe. Her feet muffled by the thickness of the carpet she went through to the sitting-room, flung off her coat, and thankfully poured herself a drink. Then she had another and another.

The clock on the mantlepiece, imprisoned under its glass

dome, endlessly wriggled its brass cogs. Time filled the room, encapsulated the house; long, lonely, loveless years of time. No amount of alcohol would ever erase the pain of them.

Wendy was gone. Instinct reared up like a monster to tell her that she would never come back. Impossible to exist in such a vacuum. Need hacked at her body like a butcher's cleaver. Holding herself together, nursing herself, she made her way upstairs. Tenderly, she opened Peter's door. Halfway inside, the smile of hope still clinging to her face, her feet faltered then stopped.

Owen and Peter were cuddled close together in one of the single beds. Owen was stroking Peter's hair. Peter's eyes were lightly, blissfully closed and there was a stiffness of rapture about him.

Chapter Twenty-nine

"Bastards!" she said. "Bastards! Bastards!"

They scrambled out of bed, naked, jerking on trousers, shirts and shoes.

A black line traced down Owen's spine and disappeared between his waxy buttocks.

"Filthy bastards!"

"You don't understand," Peter cried out.

"Sick! Sick!"

"No, it's you!"

"Me?" She sent a wild howl of laughter up to the ceiling. "You bastard!"

Owen's voice had a barely disguised tremble.

"Some things have got to be accepted, girl."

"Who says?"

"Everyone nowadays. Life it is."

"No! Sick it is! Why should you be allowed to go around contaminating other people?"

"Leave him alone," Peter said. "I love him."

She screwed up her face.

"Oh, you poor sick bastard."

"There's nothing wrong with love. It's good and unselfish and pure."

"There's something wrong with you."

An obscene travesty of a laugh was jerking high in Owen's throat.

"But why, girl? Just because he loves a man instead of a woman, is it?"

"You revolting pervert! Do you think this is funny?"

"He's not laughing," Peter protested. "It's just nerves."

"Oh, shut up, you skinny little creep. How bloody well dare you have married me? How dare you have used me to cover up your perverted little life? How dare you be so cruel and selfish? How dare you do such a thing to me, play such a trick, deny me any real normal life of my own? How bloody well dare you? People like you and your precious friend should be kept apart from ordinary people. It should be on your medical card, on something, on everything. People should know for their own protection."

"Celia, you're talking as if we're lepers. We're not infectious, you know."

"You bastard! You've ruined my life worse than any filthy bloody germ."

"Oh, come now, girl." Owen's hand shook as he lit up a cigarette. He blew smoke and crinkled eyes in which no laughter was reflected.

"Peter has been good to you. Given you every comfort."

Suddenly hilarity spiralled up through Celia's body and exploded in her throat. She choked and screamed with it. Stumbling, staggering, banging into walls and doors she eventually found her own bedroom. Once inside she locked the door and leaned against it. Then the hysterical laughter changed to wailing and weeping.

A huge wave of grief swelled up in her. She grabbed the cigarette lighter on the bedside table and thumbed the flame into quivering, thrusting life. It penetrated the bed-drapes, explored, consumed, licked deep into the bed and shot out towards curtains, cushions, walls and chairs. She retreated, breathless, her heart a fast-beating alarm.

Peter was banging on the door and screaming.

"For God's sake! Celia! Celia!"

In exquisite relief she rolled her body and her face against the wood. He did care. Caring was in his voice. This was the test. When she was in danger, he cared. Always she had known that his caring was locked away somewhere. It was only a matter of finding the right key and allowing it to be released. Coughing and choking she managed to open the door and reach the top of the stairs where she could hang onto the banister and gasp for air.

She heard Owen's voice but could not see him.

"For Christ's sake, let's get out of here!"

"The cow. The stupid cow!" Peter said. "Look what she's done to the house." He kept repeating over and over again as he went downstairs, "The stupid cow . . . the stupid useless cow . . ."

Celia followed him, confused and harried by the crackling and creaking and rustling that was growing in intensity around her. She wandered into the sitting-room and collected her coat and handbag. Peter was ringing for the fire brigade. His voice trembled and she longed to comfort him, but Owen already had his arm around him. Owen comforted him. Owen caressed him. Owen cajoled him outside to safety.

Celia walked away.

She would have a flat. She would have love.

She would have freedom. She would have love.

She would have parties. She would have love.

She would have gaiety and life and laughter.

And somewhere, from somebody—she would have love.